THE TALE OF NEFRET

By

M.L. Bullock

I dedicate this book to Luke Broadhead, my nephew, blacksmith, archaeologist-in-training and professional brainstormer. I have three words for you, "To the swords!"

I am your darling sister.
I am to you like a bit of land,
With each shrub of grateful fragrance.
Lovely is the water-conduit in it,
Which your hand has dug,
While the north wind cooled us.
A beautiful place to wander,
Your hand in my hand,
My soul inspired,
My heart in bliss,
Because we go together.

Egyptian poem, 2000 BC

Prologue

Egypt—18th Dynasty

Farrah stood outside the door of the tent and stared up into the night sky. No matter how heavily time etched cruel marks on her face, the view grabbed her breath as if her dark eyes were seeing it for the first time. The lines on her brown face deepened as she pursed her lips. The air around her was pregnant with the future, but her inner sight was dark and full of mystery. Her limited insight into the other world made her uncomfortable. She made the sign of peace to the Dancing Man that hung above her in purple blackness as he rose above the tribal camp. The Cushite traders called the Dancing Man a different name—Osiris he was called in the Black Lands and beyond—but here in the Red Lands where the red sands swirled and swam about the desert people like a dead ocean, he was known as the Dancing Man.

How long will we travel this path? An endless caravan moving from one rain oasis to another? Many of the clan no longer know from whence they came or that there had once been a place for them. How many Meshwesh must die in the Red Lands before we see those white walls again?

Once the Meshwesh dwelled in a city of white stone, Zerzura. What a city it had been! Farrah could barely remember the feeling of cool stones under her feet, the tastes of orange fruit sweet on her tongue, and the many pools of clear blue water that her young body had swum in. Had it been just a dream? No, Farrah remembered the day when the cowardly old king, Onesu, had fled the city ahead of the horde of giants who rushed in to claim it. But he had not lived one day after he left Zerzura, for Farrah had cut his throat while he slept. When he awoke to see her face above him, she whispered why she had done it as she watched him bleed. He had lost the city and had abandoned Ze, his queen and Farrah's sister, leaving her to the pleasure of the giants who no doubt raped her to death. Farrah shuddered inwardly thinking of what she had done. Nobody knew, yet it was a spot on her soul. She did not regret it, although the gods had seen fit to take her inner sight from her as punishment for her crime. That had been long, long ago. His face no longer haunted her. Yet often she imagined she heard Ze's screams in the clear night.

Now, with a silent prayer Farrah considered again the stars above her. Regardless of the constellation's name, this sour omen was an inauspicious sign for the birth of a royal child, but there was nothing she could do to prevent it. Even her magic could not stop a child who wanted to enter this realm.

Farrah suddenly felt old. Had she, leader of the Council of Old Ones, become too old to consider the deeper meaning of such things? Was she too old to help bring another baby into this increasingly difficult world? The sounds the mother made, the painful moaning, the calling of her name, let Farrah know that she indeed still had a purpose. She took a deep sigh, breathing in the warm desert air and shaking off the unseen trepidation. She tossed her head cloth to the ground. No heads covered this night. She smiled peacefully as she walked to the birthing bed and looked down into the face of the beautiful Kadeema.

What a beauty the young queen had been when she first arrived here as the bride to Semkah! However, the Red Lands had sapped away her pretty softness like it did to all women who were not of true Red Lands' blood. She had become hard, hard like the clay that lay beneath the rough sand. Kadeema's olive skin was no longer pale but red, and her hair no longer like bright copper but dark and dull. The young queen's eyes still had their sea-green beauty, but the sparkle, the joy of love and living, had faded. A wife of a young tribal king tied to the Red Lands people only by the most tenuous of threads—love. Farrah looked into those eyes, saddened to see that where there had been hope and excitement, there was now fear and regret.

When Kadeema arrived, the people had loved her, celebrating her light skin and unusual eyes with poems and songs. She had been like a child—a treasure to them, for the tribe treasured children above all things. Their young prince needed a bride, and why should he not take a beautiful bride like Kadeema? She was the daughter of a faraway Grecian king who was a friend to the tribe, so it was a good match.

Semkah was not a king like his brother Omel, who was fierce, strong and brave yet crafty and changeable. Semkah was steady and ever obedient to the Council, trusting them in all things that concerned the Meshwesh. Omel never displayed such devotion.

Semkah wore the tribal king's robes early after the death of his father, but he cut a fine figure even as a young man. Farrah remembered that day. She'd watched as his arms were tattooed with the sign of the tribe, the falcon's wings with a swirl of sand wrapped around it. He had worn his hair long, with two long braids at his temples. His chest gleamed with turquoise and gold necklaces from the mines of the Meshwesh, and at his wrist were the slender snake bracelets that only kings wore.

The young king's older brother Omel had an unabashed love for all things Egyptian. He wore linen Egyptian tunics that showed his scrawny, tanned legs. Tall and thin, Omel kept his dark hair shaved and his head shone with oils. Sometimes he wore a folded cloth on his head, but always his eyes were lined with black, as if he were an Egyptian royal. There was no doubt amongst the Council that Omel loved the Black Lands and would abandon his heritage if given a chance. But for that, he needed his brother. Semkah and Omel had received a divided inheritance—a smart and seemingly prophetic move by their wily father, Onesu. Semkah held the turquoise mines and Omel the gold, but they shared a workforce and the resources required to continue the work. Farrah suspected that Omel would seek to correct this. Already he drew men to his side like flies to a sweet fruit. She wondered what he promised them.

The brothers had different ideas about the future of the clan. Omel wanted with much passion to bring them into Egypt's good graces. Farrah spat on the ground at the thought of such nonsense. Semkah's dream was different—he dreamed of reclaiming Zerzura, as was his right, but he had no way of accomplishing that. No more than his father had.

Omel often met with Semkah and other tribal leaders to try to rally them to his point of view. "We need Egypt, brothers! They have wealth beyond measure and green lands that are just waiting for our plows. Come with me to Egypt and meet with Huya. He has given me his oath that Pharaoh wants to honor us with these lands." Semkah had laughed at this idea and made no secret that he wanted no part of Omel's Egyptian ways.

"And what will Pharaoh require, brother?" Semkah had said with a patient smile that only further angered Omel. "The king of Egypt does not simply give away lands to appease his neighbors. What of our inheritance? Have you given up finding our homeland, all for a bag of beans from Egypt's hand? I know what it will require, and that I cannot do. Pharaoh will take our mines, our cattle—maybe even our wives and children—and for what? Some soggy ground so wet that only mosquitos dwell there? How can you ask this of me? What do I say to my tribe?"

Omel had scowled but said nothing else on the matter at that time. Farrah did not think any of the Council or the other leaders believed they had heard the last of Omel's desires. But Semkah never saw the dark side of his brother; he only recognized the good. He had a heart of gold.

Farrah mumbled to herself remembering the night Semkah was born. What were the words she had said over him as she cradled him on that first night? "He will pursue love from one end of the desert to another. He will give his life for love, and that is the noblest of deaths."

That had been her proclamation then. She wondered what the hidden words would be tonight or if her old ears would even hear them. She shook her head, reminding herself to stay in the present; she had a habit of getting lost in the past so many times lately. With authority, she flipped up the dress of the writhing Kadeema. She prayed and swayed, calling on her ancestors to assist her.

"No! Do not call on them. They must not know...!" Kadeema shouted savagely.

Farrah could not help but shudder. In her madness, Kadeema could offend a wandering spirit or worse. Farrah made a secret sign to ward off evil curses. Before she could protest further, Kadeema's womb burst forth blood and she screamed into the musky night. Farrah nodded and prayed silently as she examined the woman's body.

Something was amiss. Ignoring Kadeema's scream, she probed inside her with expert fingers and felt the baby's head. No! Inside the queen were two babies, two lives struggling to emerge into this world. Without knowing how she knew, she did know—these would be the only children of Semkah and Kadeema. Before they were born, it had been prophesied that from Semkah's tribe would come the mekhma, the leader who would carry them home. Farrah felt an excitement greater than the fear, an urgency like none she had experienced before. These children must be born!

Kadeema screamed again as the children turned, each fighting to emerge first from their mother's womb. The sharp scent of birthing blood filled the tent, and Farrah sniffed. Did she smell death? Ah, yes, it lingered there, just beyond the gathered crowd.

She rubbed her hand with oil and soothed the expectant mother, numbing Kadeema to the pain with expert movements. Quietly Farrah called Mina, her acolyte. "Listen to what I say. Go about the camp and untie all the knots. No one must wear anything that is knotted. It is a bad omen for this birth, for this night. Do as I tell you, Mina!" Mina, who rarely spoke, nodded and touched her forehead as a sign of respect, and then fled from the tent. Farrah heard a hush fall over the camp; even the animals were mute. Farrah went about the tent untying everything she could find as Semkah watched her nervously. Finally, she untied Kadeema's gown and covered her with a blanket. Even the braids in her hair were removed and left untied.

"What are you doing, Old One?" Semkah inquired, a worried look on his handsome face.

"No questions now," Farrah warned. Was it her fault that the king did not understand birthing magic? That by untying the strands near and around the queen she would prevent strangulation of the children on the mother's cord? She clucked at him with her teeth as she attended his wife.

The woman's breathing quickened, her birth pains coming more strongly now.

Ten minutes later, Kadeema's water seeped out of her and the birth began in earnest. Kadeema leaned forward in her sitting position, gripping her knees. Semkah sat behind her, whispering in her ear. Farrah could not hear the words that he spoke, but she was sure they were words of love.

That is a shame. He will not have her long.

She thought these things without ever questioning why or how she knew them. She just knew them. There was no denying that. More often than not, she was correct, but why cause anguish at such a time? A birth is a time of joy—a time to celebrate, not a time to cry and mourn. *"Ah, but mourning there shall be, and much mourning…"*

Farrah spoke the words of life as the first pink head crowned from between the mother's loins. But as quickly as it began to slide out, a tiny hand reached out and grabbed its shoulder, pulling it back inside the mother. Kadeema screamed in great pain as the second child now emerged. In amazement, Farrah watched and faithfully caught the first child to emerge from the womb. Would this be the first or the second? Who came first? She smiled at their luck—two children! She tossed the first birth rag into a nearby container. She would burn it later at a special ceremony; it was a precious and rare item to possess.

Thank you, ancestors!

The second child began to emerge. Farrah helped guide the child into this realm, cooing softly to the emerging soul. "Come out, come out now," Farrah purred to the second child. "No more fighting. You are no longer number one, but now you are number two. Let us see what you are—oh, another girl, Semkah. Two girls for you!"

Semkah's beautiful smile reflected his full heart. He had come to the tent dressed for receiving a new princess or prince, a royal child—he was now doubly blessed. No man had ever loved a woman more than Semkah loved Kadeema. And although it would have benefited him and his tribe a great deal if he had married a daughter of the Red Lands, he would have no one but the princess he met in a faraway land. He kissed his daughters' foreheads, even before Mina and Farrah cleaned them, and then turned his attention to his wife.

"Girls, Kadeema. Fine girls!"

Semkah's wife smiled weakly, shallow grooves appearing briefly at the sides of her mouth. She was too thin, too gaunt, but her vivid green eyes showed her emotion so clearly. Hers was the face of weary happiness.

Until...

As Farrah wrapped the second child in linen and wiped the blood from her skin with a damp cloth, a strange thing happened. Two birds flew into the musky desert tent. The flap had been opened slightly so the well-wishers could pray for and sing to Kadeema as she gave birth to the treasures of the tribe.

The larger bird, a falcon, swooped and screeched as it circled the inside of the tent, chasing the smaller bird with reckless ferocity. The larger bird, a Heret falcon, was a rare sight this far out into the Red Lands but not unheard of. His prey was much rarer—it was the green Bee-Eater, a tiny bird that found bees as tasty as humans did honey. At Zerzura, the Bee-Eater would have been a welcome sight—it was, after all, the Oasis of the Little Birds. No bird was smaller than the Bee-Eater. The falcon screamed in the tent as it crashed into Farrah's collection of ivory idols, unlit candles and various bowls of dried herbs and flowers. A surprised Kadeema protected her daughters from the melee by waving her hands at the birds. Semkah captured the falcon easily with a cloth, but the Bee-Eater escaped out of the tent, ducking the reaching hands and makeshift snares. Semkah took the falcon outside—it was wrapped in the cloth that had become the creature's net.

The king opened the cloth to release the bird, but it did not take to the wind. On closer inspection, it had a bloody wing and seemed unable to fly. Semkah covered it back up, intending to cage it until the injuries healed—then he would set it free. Before he could argue or protest, Farrah reached for the bundle. Her faded dark eyes appraised the animal astutely, and then she gripped it and twisted its neck until it snapped.

"Why? Why did you do this, Farrah? I could have saved it."

"You would try, but you could not. Now it is dead and you are alive. See to your wife, now. She needs you." Farrah felt tired—too tired to explain to the king the hidden meaning of her actions.

Semkah jutted out his square jaw. The two turned to walk back into the tent and were surprised to find Kadeema standing nearly naked and bloody at the tent entrance. The people had pushed back and were standing close to the fire in the center of the camp. They whispered, wondering what the omen of the birds meant.

The Dancing Man above us, the birds in the tent, twins? What did it all mean?

Farrah heard what they said. Feeling their eyes upon her, she waved her hands, easily capturing their attention. With purposeful steps she walked toward the fire and stared into the flames. She saw nothing—nothing but shadows—yet the words formed easily on her tongue. Prophecy began to bubble up from deep within, somewhere beneath her navel. Each utterance was her offspring, birthed from within her, rare seeds planted there issuing from her ancestors, or perhaps from the gods themselves.

"Peace, sons and daughters of Ma. Tonight is a night to be remembered, for we have been doubly blessed..." Farrah wanted to bring hope and encouragement to help the tribe see that the arrival of the two girls was nothing to be feared, but other words burst forth and would not be held back.

"Two destinies have been born tonight, Meshwesh! You have a choice! Follow the Old Ways or fall under the shadow of death and be lost forever!" The crowd gasped and stirred uncomfortably in the sand. Farrah's mind futilely grappled with what to say. The seer inside her would speak unfiltered. *"Evil arises from the sand... who can be saved? Ah, I see it!"* She screamed despite her mind's instruction to remain calm. The images of a great battle spanned before her; many Meshwesh perished before the golden swords of giant beasts of men. *"Two mekhmas—two paths, Meshwesh. One will lead you to safety behind the white walls of Zerzura, and the other to a future unknown. You saw the Heret pursue the Bee-Eater—so shall one child chase the other. What will be your fate, Meshwesh? Will you disappear into the red sand?"* A dry laugh escaped Farrah's lips as she fought for control of her own mind. She spoke words in a language she could not comprehend.

Semkah put out his hands to his wife, intending to hold her and wrap her in his arms, but she let out a bloodcurdling scream—and she didn't stop screaming. There were no words spoken, only an agonizing cry that came from deep within her soul. Her eyes were wide and full of unspoken, unknowable fear. Farrah helped Semkah place her back in the bed. She fought them at first, pointing and staring at something no one else could see. Finally he calmed her and she allowed Farrah to place her in her covers and pat away the blood. Semkah held her shaky hand, wept, and cajoled, but he could not coax her to speak to him.

For days, Kadeema spoke not a word to any living soul. Farrah stayed with her, watching over her, feeding her, but still she never spoke. Farrah knew what this was. Kadeema had had a vision—a vision of the future. Farrah suspected that Kadeema had the gift all along, but the younger woman was obviously untrained and unaware that she could do and see such things. Since her vision had undoubtedly occurred when Farrah and Semkah had been dealing with the birds, it must have been a vision concerning her daughters. For Farrah, this was impossible to bear. She had to know what hovered just beyond the veil in the other realm.

Quietly she called Mina to her and gave her a list of flowers and roots to find. She would need these things if she was to stir Kadeema's memory. A few hours later, her dark-skinned acolyte returned with the things Farrah had requested. Again, Mina made the sign of respect and walked out of the tent backwards. Farrah stoked the fire in one of the firepots. She snatched strands of Kadeema's hair out by the root and tossed them on the fire. The mystified Kadeema hardly flinched. Next, Farrah tossed the items Mina had brought her into the low flame and slowly said the words of power as she did so.

She waved a small branch of shrubby rose over the smoke and waved it again over Kadeema to cleanse the young woman's mind. Using the smoke had some risks, but not to Farrah—only to Kadeema. She had seen that

Kadeema would die soon, and perhaps this would hasten her passing, but that was a risk Farrah had to take. The future of the Meshwesh could depend on this! Sometimes, the smoke led a person into the dream world never to return, but Farrah suspected that Kadeema was there already. She was lost in a world of visions. How Farrah envied her! Since she'd taken the life of Onesu, she could not see fully. Now she strained and muttered, sometimes inaccurately, sharing what she saw in the flames or in the water.

Kadeema breathed in the fumes and soon was sitting up on the bed, staring harder at whatever it was she saw in the smoke.

"What do you see, Kadeema? Tell me!"

The queen began talking, low at first, then louder and more clearly. "I see a city far in the desert—hidden away from the eyes of men." Kadeema's voice, small and timid, reflected her wonder at what she saw. "Nothing there now, nothing but shadows…shadows of the fallen ones." She began to shake, and her lip quivered. "Ah…I am so cold."

Farrah ignored her and pushed her to share more. "Tell me, Semkah's wife. What do you see now? Can you see the fountain? What about the tower? Are any fires burning there? I must know!"

To Farrah's surprise, Kadeema laughed at her. "So you wish to go back? You've forgotten the way, haven't you, Old One?"

For a moment, it was as if Farrah could hear a different voice speaking, a familiar voice. She felt her mouth go dry, and her eyes widened.

"There is no path back for you, Far-rah. What is done is done."

"Ze? Sister?" Farrah's hand shook with excitement. "Speak to me, sister!"

Kadeema's face changed. The spirit of Ze had passed by, leaving the slack-faced queen behind. She mumbled, "My daughters! I see them! My beautiful girls! How much they look like me!"

She got up on her knees, staring into the smoke, mesmerized by whatever it was she saw. "One will overtake the other! See? See them? How cruel you are, Farrah—you spoke the words. Now look! Can you see them? My daughters!" Kadeema began to cry softly in the smoky tent. Farrah feared that someone would hear the queen's cries.

"Now, now, my queen. All will be well." Her hands still trembling, she smoothed the queen's tangled hair.

"I cannot stay here, Farrah. I cannot stay and see what shall become of my daughters. You cannot have them both, Old One." Farrah could see Kadeema's awareness returning. The power of the smoke was fading. "You cannot kill them both."

Farrah drew her hand back in shock. "I would never do such a thing! Children are treasures of the tribe!"

Kadeema gripped the older woman's hands and stared at them. "So you say, but you lie! They shall both rule. Ah…but then…" A sigh came from the depths of her heart. "I see blood on your hands, Old One! I have seen what you have done."

Farrah's eyes narrowed. How could she know? Could she have seen Farrah slide the blade across Onesu's neck in the clouds of smoke? Before she knew what to say or do, the queen commanded, "Kill me, with your sharp blade! The one you have hidden there in the box. Slide it under my chin and into my brain, Farrah! Please do not leave me in my misery, for I know you shall kill my daughters." She clutched Farrah's hand desperately, her green eyes rivers of pain and hopelessness.

"How can you ask me to do this? You speak like a madwoman, Kadeema." Farrah stood, pushing away from the grasping queen. She gathered her thoughts as Kadeema wept. She had little patience for talking more with the young woman. The queen's mind was feverish, lost—that's what Farrah would say. No one would believe Kadeema.

"Sit, rest, eat. You will feel better soon. Stay here, and I will fetch your husband for you. Semkah has been caring for your daughters, but I suspect that his heart is truly with you. Let me find him." Farrah had to leave; she had to consult the Council on what to do next. She had pledged never to take another life, and so she would not, despite what the queen might believe.

Kadeema did not look at her but stared off into her dreamland with her own private vision. "Yes, I shall wait—for a little while."

Only a brief time had passed when Farrah and Semkah returned. Semkah's handsome smile quickly disappeared, and his dark looks clouded with concern. "Wife?" When she didn't answer, he turned to Farrah and frowned. "Where is she?"

Farrah couldn't hide her surprise. "She was here in her bed, my king. She had a vision! A vision of your daughters!" Quickly she lied, "She asked me to find you. Could I deny her the presence of the king?"

"Why would you leave her?" He growled at Farrah, careful not to strike her as he might like to. "Kadeema? Kadeema? Are you here?" Semkah called again and again. Soon the entire camp was summoned and the search began in earnest. By the time a search party took to the desert sands, the wise woman knew in her bones that Kadeema was dead or very near it. The herbs had increased Farrah's ability to see, if only for a little while. She knew because she could see Kadeema now, glimpses of her. Farrah didn't bother to seek for her; she would never be able to find her, only see her in her mind's eye. Farrah stared into the darkness and watched the queen.

Kadeema walked as far as she could, lay down in the sand, and allowed it to wash over her. Her beautiful eyes focused on a point in the dark sky; the Dancing Man careened above her. With her last breath she shook herself, realizing with sadness how she'd come to be lying in the perilous sands of the Sahara. The queen did not fight her fate, for she had chosen it—finally, for one instant in her life, she showed courage. *No sense in fighting now, Kadeema. You now die, and that is your fate.*

Farrah tried to remain aloof, unmoved by the picture of the lovely upturned face disappearing beneath the red sands, her thin bloody gown fluttering around her frail body. Yes, she had loved the girl. How could one not love a beautiful face and cheery laugh? Still, Kadeema had saved Farrah the trouble of silencing her.

You have blood on your hands, Old One!

How foolish to think that Farrah would kill the treasures of the tribe, the daughters of Semkah. The queen had been wrong, surely. A small voice inside her whispered, "Yes, you would. You would do even that to go home."

Surprised by her own thoughts, an unexpected wave of sadness washed over Farrah as the queen's soul slipped from the earth's realm.

Suddenly, she yelled at the queen, "Stand! Rise, now— before it is too late!" But the green eyes did not see Farrah; they saw nothing now.

Semkah never found her.

Chapter One

Rivalry—Nefret

Clapping my hands three times, I smiled, amused at the half-dozen pairs of dark eyes that watched me entranced with every word and movement I made. "And then she crept up to the rock door and clapped her hands again…" *Clap, clap, clap.* The children squealed with delight as I weaved my story. This was one of their favorites, The Story of Mahara, about an adventurous queen who constantly fought magical creatures to win back her clan's stolen treasures.

"Mahara crouched down as low as she could." I demonstrated, squatting as low as I could in the tent. "She knew that the serpent could only see her if she stood up tall, for he had very poor eyesight. If she was going to steal back the jewel, she would have to crawl her way into the den, just as the serpent opened the door. She was terrified, but the words of her mother rang in her ears: 'Please, Mahara! Bring back our treasures and restore our honor!'"

I crawled around, pretending to be Mahara. The children giggled. "Now Mahara had to be very quiet. The bones of a hundred warriors lay in the serpent's cave. One wrong move and that old snake would see her and…catch her!" I grabbed at a nearby child, who screamed in surprise. Before I could finish my tale, Pah entered our tent, a look of disgust on her face.

"What is this? Must our tent now become a playground? Out! All of you, out! Today is a special day, and we have to get ready."

The children complained loudly, "We want to hear Nefret's story! Can't we stay a little longer?"

Pah shook her head, and her long, straight hair shimmered. "Out! Now!" she scolded the spokesman for the group.

"Run along. There will be time for stories later," I promised them.

As the heavy curtain fell behind them, I gave Pah an unhappy look. She simply shook her head. "You shouldn't make promises that you may not be able to keep, Nefret. You do not know what the future holds."

"Why must you treat them so? They are only children!" I set about dressing for the day. Today we were to dress simply with an aba—a sleeveless coat and trousers. I chose green as my color, and Pah wore blue. I cinched the aba at the waist with a thick leather belt. I wore my hair in a long braid. My fingers trembled as I cinched it with a small bit of cloth.

"Well, if nothing else, you'll be queen of the children, Nefret."

I smoothed wisps of curly hair with both hands as I stared at my reflection in the brass mirror. "Then it's settled. I'll rule the children and you can have the adults." I smiled at her, hoping one last time to make peace with her. It wasn't to be. With an eye roll she exited the tent, and I stepped out behind her to greet the day.

My stomach growled. I was ready to break my fast. I could smell the bread baking on the flames. Although banished from my tent earlier, "my" children—Ziza,

Amon and Paimu—followed me. Ziza and Amon were born Meshwesh, but the tribe had adopted Paimu.

Many seasons ago, a small band of stragglers from the Algat came to trade with us. When they left early in the morning, they left Paimu behind. My father had been convinced that it was an oversight and that the Algat would return to claim their daughter, but they did not. Paimu was now everyone's child, but secretly I pretended that she was mine.

"You will win today, Nefret! You will win and be the mekhma!" She whooped and danced around me, and the other two children, her followers, imitated her. I hissed at her playfully as Pah stomped away.

"Stop that now—you'll jinx me. Have you eaten? Where is your breakfast, Paimu?" I knew she had not. The little girl with the black curls ate like a bird.

"I shall eat with you."

"Not today, little one. I have to eat with Semkah."

"Oh, I see." Her bottom lip protruded, and I tousled her curls.

"But when I am done, I shall look for you. You want to climb that tree today? You think you are strong enough?"

"Strong like a monkey!" Paimu pretended to scratch under her arms and played at being a monkey. We had seen many of the nasty animals in the past few months. The traders loved to bring them to us as if we'd never seen them before, parading them around in golden chains. Despite my aversion, I felt great sympathy for the animals. Nothing deserved to be chained. "Can't we do it now? Before you go eat?"

I paused on the path, and people jostled past us. The camp was full today; I had been so consumed with my own thoughts that I hardly noticed the arrival of my uncle's people. Their green and yellow costumes were everywhere. Many of them greeted me, smiling, and the gold about their necks glinted in the early morning light. I felt my stomach twist, and I gladly accepted Paimu's excuse to put off breakfast. "Only a few minutes, though. I dare not keep the king waiting."

"Okay then!" Paimu and the other two children hopped and skipped around me like happy goats. I laughed at their playfulness. We walked to the edge of the camp, where the palm trees swayed above a pool of clear blue water. Our temporary home, the Timia Oasis, was my favorite of all the oases that our tribes visited. Lush and green, oranges and pomegranates hung everywhere. Clusters of dates, vegetables and fresh herbs grew abundantly. Every time we left Timia, my heart broke a little. To me this was home, not distant Zerzura, although I would never confess that to anyone.

I skipped down the path with the children until we came to the tree that Paimu had been trying unsuccessfully to climb. As we entered the clearing, my heart sank. There under the tallest tree was Pah, her back propped against the curved trunk and Alexio laughing over her, touching her hair. I would have preferred to turn and walk away, but I had promised Paimu. I avoided making eye contact and helped Paimu tie up her skirt so she could climb.

I knelt down beside her, tucking the fabric neatly in the cord at her waist. "You remember what I told you? Don't look down. Take your time but keep moving. If you move too slowly, your arms will tire and you will fall."

"I won't forget, princess."

"No princess. Just Nefret." I tweaked her nose and walked with her to the tree.

"Okay, Nefret. I can do this."

"I know you can, Paimu."

Like many times before, Paimu skimmed easily up the first five feet of the tree. I talked to her patiently and soon, Alexio was climbing the tree next to hers, demonstrating his technique as she watched.

"That trunk is too large for her to grasp." Pah suddenly stood beside me, frowning up at the dark-haired girl above us. "She will hurt herself, Nefret."

"Nonsense. She's just climbing a tree, and she'll never go high enough to hurt herself."

"This isn't about you, Nefret. Get her down."

"Leave her, Pah!"

"Fine! Let her fall, then. It's no matter to me." Pah turned to walk away from the whole scene.

Nervously, I called up to the girl. "That's high enough, Paimu. Come down, brave girl." Alexio scampered down his tree, walked toward the trunk of Paimu's tree and patted it.

"Look how far I've climbed." Paimu climbed higher and higher until I could see only her feet. Ziza and Amon clapped and cheered her on.

"Look at you, Paimu! You did it! Now come down. Slowly now. Use your entire body." I truly had begun to feel frightened for her.

"Okay," Paimu yelled down, her voice unsteady and unsure. I gasped as I watched her tiny body slide down the tree. Ziza screamed, and I raced to the trunk.

"Stop, Paimu! Be still for a moment. Don't look down—stop looking down!"

"Okay," she said, her voice cracking with fear.

"I told you this would happen." Pah hadn't left; she lingered behind me.

Aggravated, I spun on my heel. "Yes, you did. Thank you, Pah." Alexio stripped off his jacket and sandals again and prepared to climb the tree, but I stopped him. "No, she's my responsibility. I will get her down." Alexio smiled patiently, giving me a mock bow. At least he didn't argue with me, and for that I was thankful. I kicked off my shoes and began to climb.

"I am coming up, my monkey girl. Be still. Are you secure?"

"Yes, but my arms are shaky, princess—I mean Nefret. I can't hold on. I am scared." I climbed as quickly as I could in an attempt to reach her; the tree shook beneath me.

"No! Stop!" she screamed, attracting more attention to our situation.

"I cannot leave you there, Paimu. What will the birds say? Now hold on while I come closer."

"What is your plan? To fall out of the tree with her?" Pah mocked us from the ground. I heard Alexio scold her, but I kept my attention on the little girl above me.

"See how clever you are. You climbed very high, but now we have to come down. I am going to move very slowly, okay? Why don't you climb down to me and meet me halfway? Then this poor old tree won't shake so much."

"I can't!"

"Yes, you can. You can do it. I am going to move up now just a tiny bit. Hold still."

I eased up the tree another short space. I did this again and again until I could reach out and touch her dirty foot.

"No, no! Please. I will fall."

"No, Paimu. I will not allow you to fall. I am the princess, remember? What I say has to be, right?"

"I guess so."

"It is so. Now I am going to climb up next to you, and you are going to hang around my shoulders like my little monkey, okay? Together we will climb down."

"I will try."

"No, you can do it."

"Careful, Nefret," someone called up to me, but I didn't answer. I had to stay focused on my task. The sweat crept across my brow, and I felt the muscles in my arms and legs burn.

"Come now. Here I am. See?" I smiled at her, but she didn't return my smile.

"I'm afraid! I am going to fall!"

"Nonsense. Here's what I want you to do. First, I am going to inch a little closer, but I will not touch you. You will put this leg around my waist and then scoop your arm under my armpit. That way, you won't fall."

"Can you hold me?"

"Of course I can. A little monkey like you is easy to carry. Take your time now. Here I come." I inched closer, my hands sweating. What would I do if something happened to Paimu, if she fell out of this tree and it was my fault? "Now first your leg. It's okay, take your time." Paimu held her breath and put her leg around my waist. She was so small that I barely felt the weight of her. "No, not around my neck. You can't choke me. Under my arm, please. Yes, that's it."

In half a minute she was on my back, and I began our descent. As I made my way down, a strand of long copper hair dangled irritatingly in my face. I couldn't help but notice that half the camp had come to witness the rescue but Pah had disappeared. Once we got a few feet from the ground, Paimu threw herself off my back and into Alexio's waiting arms. My tribe clapped at the happy ending before they walked away to attend to their chores and various jobs.

I stood grinning at Paimu. "Good job, little monkey. Next time, though, don't climb so high." I kissed her head, and she went running back down the path to find her friends. "Thank you for your help, Alexio."

"I was happy to provide it. You'll make a monkey out of her yet. Although I don't think your sister appreciated the show. Aren't you expected at your father's table this morning?"

My eyes widened. "Oh no! I have to go! Thank you again!" I ran down the path, his playful laughter in my ears.

Father's colorful tent was at the center of the camp. It was easy to spot—the falcon banner, the symbol of our tribe, flew over the top of it. I walked through the crowded camp, greeting those who greeted me without stopping too long for small talk. A few of my uncle's tribe openly sneered at me; it was no secret that they hoped Pah would become the mekhma. I wasn't sure why, but it was no matter to me. I had no skill at politics and no desire to seek support from anyone. I stepped inside the tent and was immediately greeted by Mina.

Farrah's acolyte greeted me silently with a demure smile and a bowl of fresh water. Quickly, I sloshed water over my hands as was the custom before dining with the king. The tent was full of dignitaries, including our uncle Omel and his sons except Alexio, his youngest. I took my seat to the left of our father; Pah always sat at his right during these official visits. We sat cross-legged around a low round table that was heaped with food. I stared at the tempting wheel of cheese near me, but I didn't dare partake until Father did. The king always took his food first. Father had the bearing of a king, or so I believed. He dressed in his royal blue tunic with the gold hand stitching around the hem. His dark brown hair was oiled and braided, and it hung down his back. He wore no jewelry today; his arm tattoos shone, and I imagined I could see them twist around his arms like living snakes. I shook myself, reminding myself to stay present in the moment.

Looking around the room, I recognized most of the faces. Sitting exactly opposite of our father was his brother Omel, another Meshwesh tribal leader. Omel's tribe and ours migrated from one rain oasis to the next as our people had done since we'd lost Zerzura to the Nephal, the giants who came down from their homeland far to the north. The giants believed this was their land, although Egypt's kings had defeated them a lifetime ago. Occasionally, they still made incursions into the Red Lands to murder, terrorize and rape our women. After they took Zerzura, they disappeared again, but not before hiding the city in the sand first. Or at least that was the story we were told.

I shivered, feeling as if someone were staring at me. I looked around the room and saw that it was Farrah, the Old One, the head of the Council. Her lips were pursed as she seemed to look right through me. I shivered again and crossed my fingers behind my back to prevent her from reading my mind. With those dark piercing eyes, I suspected that she had the power to stare into my soul.

Our father was king, but the Council acted as the spiritual leaders of all the Meshwesh. They heard various matters concerning inheritance and sickness, and they settled property disputes. They were wise and learned and could detect a lie before it was told, or so they told us. Truthfully, kings did not hold much power in our clan. Naturally, they were the leaders of our clan when there was no mekhma, but beyond protecting the people and developing military strategies, their powers were limited.

For a millennium, the Meshwesh were ruled by the mekhmas, wise young women selected by the Council of Old Ones. According to the legends, many had special magical powers bestowed upon them by the gods they served, and the king and clan served the mekhma with their lives—if it was so required. My mother had been no mekhma—she was born in a faraway land called Grecia. She served as the king's consort only—the Meshwesh had not had a mekhma since Ze, the sister of Farrah who died during the flight from Zerzura.

I smiled at Farrah to stop her staring and began doing some studying of my own. There was much to see here today in our camp. Thankfully, there were no monkeys or tigers, no traders telling us fantastic stories. How many hoped that by doing so we would divulge the location of our sacred gold and turquoise mines? No Meshwesh would ever do such a thing.

I watched our uncle; I could see that he did not defer to his people in anything. I suspected he had no desire to have a mekhma to lead him. He wanted nothing but to be king—and to convince his brother to make a lasting peace with Egypt. To this suggestion, our father always laughed. And despite the seriousness of today's gathering, Omel did not miss an opportunity to bemoan what he considered his brother's lack of foresight in regards to Pharaoh's most recent offer.

"Again, brother? I have given my answer." Our father took a handful of grapes, popped a few in his mouth and handed the bowl to Omel, who accepted it. He did not take any grapes but put the bowl back on the low cedar table with an odd thumping sound. Omel wasn't satisfied.

"Hear me out, Semkah. This is what our father would have wanted! Peace and safety for the Meshwesh. I have it on good authority that Egypt is willing to give us lands—lands of our own! No more traveling the sands, brother, searching for a lost city! We can be a nation again with a strong defense—walls to protect us." When Father didn't answer him, Omel continued with his plea. He may have thought he was convincing his brother, who said nothing, but I could have told him not to waste his time. For Father and our entire tribe, Zerzura would be our only home. Meshwesh blood had been shed there, holy blood. It would not be forgotten.

"I have been talking to the traders, brother. They say that families have disappeared, never to be seen or heard from again. Let me call Ohn in here to tell you what he saw. He's just returned from Siya, where he was to trade with the men there. Nobody was there. The oasis was empty, yet the tents remained."

Father raised his hands, his tattoos plainly showing. For the briefest of seconds, again it appeared as if the snakes were alive and writhing. I gasped and blinked as Father said, "Brother, enough of this! I will hear Ohn later, but let us tend to the things that are before us first."

Omel rose to his feet in a shot. I did not know what his intentions were, but he looked dark, very dark indeed. "You sit here in your comfortable tent while people die in the Red Lands! I tell you the Nephal have returned, and they care not for your kingship or the mekhma! We need the help of Egypt if we are going to withstand them!"

Father rose to calm him, but Farrah stood instead. "Omel! Do not disgrace these proceedings! You will have a chance to speak, just as Semkah said, but now is the time to bless your brother's daughters before they begin their trials." Omel unhappily returned to his seat but refused to look at his brother, even when he addressed him. The proceedings were long. Farrah recited the long list of mekhmas that had served the Meshwesh over the centuries. I knew them all by heart, as Pah did. Pah and I were formally introduced at *anni-mekhmas*, or queens-in-training. The leaders politely clapped for us as we stood before them. The tent grew hotter as the day went along, and there seemed to be no end to the formalities. Finally, Farrah and the others were ready to dismiss us, warning us not to discuss with the others anything that was said or done.

"These are sacred proceedings, and even as anni-mekhmas you must take care to preserve our traditions. Go now. Enjoy your final night together."

"What?" Pah and I stared at one another. "What do you mean?" I asked Farrah.

"Tonight is the last night you share a tent. Tomorrow, you begin your new life and your trials begin in earnest—we will present you to the tribe as anni-mekhmas. When you leave this tent you are no longer Nefret and Pah, sisters, daughters of Semkah. Hug one another now." We hugged awkwardly, and then Pah pulled away from me and waited silently to be excused. Farrah nodded while our father and the others clapped respectfully. Pah disappeared out the door flap and I ran after her.

Chapter Two

The Necklace—Nefret

Despite my most ardent attempts at conversation, my sister refused to speak with me beyond a few words. When we left the king's tent she ran to be with her friends and left me behind once again. I spent the rest of the day playing with the children and avoiding adult conversation as much as possible. If this was to be my last day as a child, simply a daughter of Semkah, then I would make the most of it. At the end of the day, I walked back to our tent but Pah was not there. I took my supper alone and crawled into bed, only to fall asleep waiting for her.

I did not hear her return. When I did wake, it was near morning. As usual, I awoke before Pah. I longed to push back the wheels of time so the two of us might become children again. Then I would wake her with tickles or a playful nudge. She would not bark at me or deride me for being childish. How long ago that had been! Now I dared not disturb her in such a way. "Pah, are you awake?" I whispered in the darkness. She did not answer me. I heard her soft snore. Still in the dream world; it would be cruel to wake her now.

Dread washed over me. The unknown challenges yawned before me, and my imagination began to spin fantastic tales about what things I may have to accomplish. I sighed in the darkness.

Sliding out of my pallet, I reached for my robe. Many of the gold thread tassels were missing, but I could not part with it; it had been one of the few items that belonged to my mother. Pah had Mother's braid—her princess lock—I had her robe. I slid into the comfortable garment and stepped outside through the fold in the back of the tent. I did not want to draw attention to myself.

Fingers of red light looked like a hand as the first glints of the sun stretched across the far horizon. Our herdsmen would be long gone to their destination by now. Anyone doing trade with the tribe would soon arrive. Most avoided the midday heat and chose to linger inside the tents of the Meshwesh where the air was cool and sweet.

I walked down the small hill behind our tent, digging my heels into the sand to maintain my balance. I was only a few yards from the oasis but since I could no longer see it, I might as well have been a hundred miles away. I liked the imagined distance. Sometimes I craved adventure. Oh, to be Mahara or one of the other courageous women in my stories!

As children, Pah, Alexio and I whispered long into the night, talking about the places we would go, the things we would see. Alexio had traveled to many places, including south to the gold mine and east to the edge of Thebes. The stories he told us of what he saw were hard to believe, but I could tell by the wonder in his eyes that he told us the truth. Pah and I had known only life in our camp.

Ungracefully, I climbed another sand dune. Satisfied finally that I was completely by myself and far enough away from my tribe to not be found, I pulled my mother's robe tighter around my body and lay back on the sand. The glistening stars above me were beginning to fade, threatened by the nearness of the sun.

I sighed and stared up at the distant moon. I imagined flying up, up and up, like a jinn or one of the gods, then looking down upon the earth. What would I see if I were a bird? What must it be like to see the Red Lands from the sky? I had to admit that I envied the gods and their vantage point—if they existed. I did not pray to them as I should. Or to anything at all, really.

Pah had a heart for faith, but I did not. How could I worship an invisible being that insisted on sacrifice, adoration and perpetual prayers? Some claimed to have seen a god or goddess, but I had seen nothing. According to the traders, the local deities were a jealous lot who would kill mortals on a whim to get what they wanted—which was often a human woman or a special musical instrument. Now the gods commanded that I compete with my sister to lead the tribe and the entire clan. As spokesman for the gods of the Meshwesh, Farrah should be able to tell us who it should be! Why must we go through trials? I felt angry, even rebellious as I lay in the sand.

How many times had Farrah taken me to the fire and commanded me to look? "Look harder, Nefret. Look with your mind's eye!" Despite her encouragement, I never saw a thing besides the flickering of the flames and the burning herbs. No queenly visions for me. My sister had that gift, and to me, Pah's vision was the proof I needed that the gods had made their decision. They had chosen my sister to lead. Although my spirit resisted this thought, my heart was happy. I only wanted my sister to be happy, I reminded myself. Suddenly I sat up. "That's what I'll do. I will tell them my sister should be the mekhma. Then we can end all this!" The idea suited me, and I ignored the small, still voice that said, "No! You must be queen!"

I frowned at the moon above me. "You do not control my life!" I was tempted to raise my fist at the moon, but what good would it do me? *What would you know of Nefret and Pah, moon? Do you even know who we are?* Of course, the moon said nothing to me. I dug my toes into the cool, red sand. I dug first with my big toe, and then I buried all my toes in the sand. Pah would complain later than I had strewn sand in our tent, but wasn't there always sand in the tent? You could not avoid it. I hardly noticed it anymore.

I leaned forward and put my elbows on my knees. This was a special moment, out here alone in the quiet. Today, the camp would be full of visitors come to watch Pah and me compete. My stomach twisted, and I felt another sigh rise from within me. I wiggled my toes deeper and felt something cold and foreign under my foot. I drew my toes back, afraid that a scorpion or snake was hidden there. The sand did not move, so I poked it again with my toe. It wasn't a creature. Now sitting cross-legged, I dug at the spot where my toes had been.

Suddenly a tiny whirlwind in the sand appeared; I fell back and watched as it spun. I shielded my eyes with my fingers to protect them from the spinning sand. When the whirlwind's work was complete, it simply dissolved into nothing; all was calm once more.

There! I could see something, something shiny. I touched it—it was a flat chain with the shine of gold. But it wasn't gold, at least none that I had ever seen. I tugged on the end until the full length of chain was free from the sand. Curious, I examined the necklace. It was beautifully made with exquisite, unfamiliar craftsmanship. Even in the muted darkness I could see this was a rare treasure. Hanging from the chain was an oval-shaped pendant. It was flat with inscribed images like I had never seen. I could see a snake, the sign for water—the rest I could not make out. Still, I knew I had found a precious thing. Perhaps it had fallen off one of the trader's caravans? I had no explanation for the small whirlwind that had unearthed it.

I looked about me nervously. Cupping the necklace in my hand I spun about the top of the dune. I didn't see anyone, and there was no evidence that anyone had been near recently. However, the sand shifted daily. How would I know that anyone had been here? I felt the cool metal in my hand. I would keep it, but I would keep it to myself. I grabbed my robe. My heart beat fast in my chest as I scurried back to my tent. Pah was awake and dressed but still not speaking to me. She stroked her hair with her brush and wrapped it into a neat braid. How I wanted to talk with her! To hear her speak kindly to me, but she did not. I shoved my secret treasure under my blanket and watched her balefully.

My stomach twisted again. Mina told me once—and I had heard her voice only a handful of times in my life—that there were two snakes of destiny fighting inside each of us. These snakes caused the twisting sensation. "The gods place the snakes inside your belly before you are born. As you grow, they grow, and one struggles to dominate the other. When the struggle ends, your destiny is decided." I begged to hear more, but she said nothing else. I understood none of it. The thought of snakes in my belly made me even more nervous and nauseous.

Farrah's acolyte had a soft voice, which always sounded raw and husky—probably because she rarely used it. Mina lived under a vow of silence, a vow to Ma'at. She was a master at nonverbal communication, using her facial expressions and hands to say much more than I could ever express with my storytelling. I admired the woman's quietness and calmness—two qualities I did not possess.

As I brushed the tangles from my own hair with an ivory comb, I watched Pah begin her day. She tossed spoons of fragrant incense into the hanging burner, filling the room with lush scent. She leaned close to the golden lamps and fanned herself with the thick clouds of smoke. How bitter it was to know that she prayed against me! Pah opened her cedar box and examined each of the items. Although I always made a show of not watching her, I knew each item by heart. A braid of light brown hair from our mother, a block of rare fragrant wood, a seashell given by a friendly and handsome servant of a Cushite trader and one more item that she took great pains to hide from me. It was the newest treasure in her collection—a stolen piece of blue fabric from Alexio's shirt. Something she kept after repairing a tear for him.

I felt a sad sigh rise in my chest but said nothing. My hands wove my hair into a braid, and I tied the end with a piece of leather. Pah and Alexio—I could not wrap my mind around it. She loved him, of that I was sure. At least she thought she did. Perhaps she only thought she loved him because she believed I did. Maybe she wanted to hurt me as only another woman could? How could I have predicted that our childhood friend would drive us further apart?

How did I feel about Alexio? My cousin had strong, muscular arms and legs. He ran faster than anyone I knew and was frequently called upon to carry out the wishes of the kings—both his father and mine. His dark hair, which he kept at shoulder length, hung about his face like strands of silk. His warm brown eyes seemed to grow more expressive as he grew older. His face was square, with a straight nose and proud lips, but he was always laughing at someone or something—most of the time at me. He laughed much less now. We all did. How different he was from the boy I once knew! We were no longer children, the three of us.

I pretended that I did not see Pah kiss the cloth and place it back inside the box. Didn't she know that I would gladly see her and Alexio marry, if that was the will of our tribes? Pah did not hide her affection for Alexio—her dark green eyes always sought his face. Still, that was not to be. Omel had made marriage arrangements for his son long ago and made no secret that he expected him to fulfill that obligation. That was the way it was for sons of Meshwesh kings; we women had much more freedom. Alexio's intended, Farafra, the daughter of a minor king named Walida, could refuse him, but she had expressed no intention of doing so. Rather, she was proud of her handsome prize. I thought she was an unpleasant sort of person who tended to laugh at the misfortune of others. She knew nothing about Alexio beyond the fact that he had a handsome face and strong arms.

After Pah's review of the contents of her box, she closed it and then lay on her rug, bowing at the waist. I could hear her whisper a prayer but could not hear the name of the god she entreated. Her fervent whispers filled me with sadness. As quietly as I could, I attended myself and prepared to leave her in peace.

"Why do you pretend you do not hear me? I know you are listening, Nefret." She rose from her rug, never looking in my direction.

I felt ashamed for spying. It had been wrong to do, but how could I not? Not knowing how to answer, I changed the subject. "Who do you pray to, Pah? Hathor or one of our mother's goddesses, Aphrodite or Hera, perhaps?"

She stood before the ivory basin, scooping up the water with a clean linen cloth. I did not think she heard me at first; she washed her face and arms, whispering as she did. I could see her shadow bounce against the tapestries, her movements like that of a lithe dancer. Pah had an elegance that could not be taught. I was awkward, unsure and at times even clumsy. I envied her that natural grace. Finally, she slid on her tunic.

My twin said, "Does that concern you? Does it matter to whom I pray?"

"No," I said with a sigh. "I am sorry I asked."

She slid on her gold bracelets and looked at me. "What do you pray for, Nefret?"

"You know I do not pray. Why should I pray to the gods that want to divide us? Don't you care, Pah?"

Avoiding my question she said sternly, "You *should* pray, Nefret, for today I will beat you—tomorrow I will beat you too. I will best you, and everyone will see that

I am the mekhma. You should pray that you do not fall and break your neck."

I made the sign against curses and whispered back, "Why say such things to me, Pah? I am not your enemy. I am your sister!"

"What does that mean, Nefret? Nothing! The prophecy has been spoken, and I will not give up my life for you. I will be the one to bring the Meshwesh back to Zerzura!"

Sudden awareness crept upon me. "Who has poisoned your heart against me, sister? We could rule together! We could! You cannot let Farrah or any of the Council divide us. If we stick together, we will stand. Remember your promise? We would always be together."

"The promises of a child. They mean nothing! How dare you speak so about the Old One, an elder of our tribe? Farrah sees the past and the future—she knows the way back home!"

"If she knows the way, why aren't we there?" To that, Pah said nothing. The silence between us grew, and I felt worried. Perhaps Pah had seen something! Had she seen my death? "Sister, please. Let us stand together and refuse to be divided!"

"You only say that because you know I am better than you, Nefret. I am faster and cleverer. You may have a prettier face and figure, but it takes more than that to be a strong mekhma."

As she spoke, tears slid down my face. "How can you speak to me so? What has happened between us?"

"Destiny has happened, Nefret. It is time to leave childhood behind and be women."

"All I want is your happiness, Pah. And…" My voice lowered, as if someone might hear us. "If that happiness includes Alexio I would not stand in your way."

She laughed sourly. "Ah, my happiness…why do you lie to yourself, Nefret? Do you think you have the power to give him to me? It is you he wants—at least for now. You and I both know that you would do anything to have him! How can you deny it?"

"I do deny it! How can you hate me so? What has changed between us? Tell me and I will fix it! I would gladly resign my right if you would only love me again. Please…sister."

Pah didn't argue with me. Instead she said quietly, "I will earn my right to rule, Nefret. That is why I *should* rule. I do not hate you, but I will win. That is my destiny."

"If it is your destiny, than I will gladly give you my vote."

She laughed—it was a dark, empty sound. "Always the weak one. I will not accept it. We will do things the right way. And when I have won, everyone will know I am the better choice."

I stared at her, refusing to believe what I heard.

"One more thing, Nefret…I have seen the future—I know that Alexio is not *my* fate. He is a dream only, for both of us, I think."

Her words burned a scar into my heart. I felt like one of the goats that the herdsmen branded with their hot prods. I could not remember when it all began, when we drifted apart, but this conversation was proof that Fate had had her way with us.

With a confident smile, she stalked out of our tent. I numbly finished dressing for the day. Although today was not a celebration for me, I obediently wore my silver earrings and bracelets and gold anklets. How I appeared mattered to my father and my tribe. I considered wearing my newfound necklace; it felt cool in my hand as I held it briefly. Deciding against it, I placed it inside my mother's robe, rolled the robe up snugly and tucked it in my bed. I walked outside and went to break my fast before joining the others in Father's tent.

"Morning, Isha," I greeted the older woman who handed me a small round bread from her basket.

"Morning, treasure of the tribe." She kissed my cheek, and I smiled at her. Such had been my greeting every morning for as long as I could remember, as it was for all children of the Meshwesh. Now that today was here, the last day of my childhood, it suddenly occurred to me that I would never hear it again. Staring at the bread in my hands, I was swept up in the emotions of the moment.

"No need to rush, princess. The Council meeting has been postponed for a little while. Surprising news from Siya." Alexio's hand was upon my shoulder. "Are you going to eat that? I'm starving."

"What? Postponed why? What happened in Siya?" With a nod to Isha, we walked away and I tore the bread in half. "Here, greedy one." Relief washed over me. I wouldn't have to face Pah now—at least not for a little while.

"Someone has been raiding the outposts along the Great Oasis of Siya. The messenger from Siya said that warriors have been seen riding there."

"Warriors? Who could it be? Is this messenger reliable?" We strolled through the camp to the pool where Paimu had raced up the tree the day before.

"I think so. He seems level-headed enough. I've spoken to him before but not today. He was ushered into Semkah's tent as soon as he climbed off his camel."

"I see." I chewed on the soft bread and wondered what this could mean. "Have you seen Pah this morning?"

"After she was turned away at the tent? No. She didn't speak to me. I get the feeling that she's angry with me."

"Pah is mad at the world. Especially me," I added. We sat at the side of the pool and finished our bread. For a long while neither of us spoke.

Finally, Alexio said fiercely, "You have to win, Nefret. No matter what! You have to win."

"I don't want to win, Alexio. I want to have my sister back."

He sighed, tossing the last of his crumbs on the water. Hungry fish sucked up the tidbits quickly and lingered near the surface hoping for more. The palm trees beside us creaked in the early morning breeze. He wanted to say something but didn't.

"You think I am stupid for hoping so, don't you?"

"No, I do not think you are stupid, but surely you can see that that time has passed. There is more at stake than your sister's feelings and your own. You think that if you don't try, Pah will love you again; that if you don't fight for your right to lead, Pah will welcome you back with open arms. You are wrong, my friend. With all her heart, Pah wants to be the mekhma. Nothing you say will change that. Even if you were to give up your right to compete—and you cannot—you could not please her."

"She said as much this morning." Feeling sorry for the golden fish, I tossed small pieces of bread in the water. "Why does it have to be like this? Why can't we serve together? Surely that is better for the people!"

In a burst of emotion he said, "Why won't you fight, Nefret? Fight for your people! Fight for your right, for Paimu—and for me? You are not a coward! You are strong with a bow, fast on your feet. And you have wisdom, a deeper wisdom than your sister! You say all you want is to keep your sister, but the truth is you are hiding, Nefret—hiding from your destiny! You are afraid, and your fear brings us no honor."

His outburst shocked me. He had never spoken so frankly with me, at least not concerning Pah. I felt as if I had been slapped. "You're asking me to give up my sister. You can't ask me to do that."

He stood and glared down at me. "I am asking nothing of you except that you try. Pah is already lost to you, Nefret." Frustrated, I called after him, but he walked away and did not look back.

Chapter Three

The Old Ways—Nefret

I observed the fish darting back and forth as they hoped more crumbs would fall into the water. They tapped at one another with their noses, jostling for a better position. I understood them. How perfect life had been just a few minutes ago when there were no crumbs in the water to disturb their peaceful world! Now that they had had a taste of bread, they thought of nothing else. They were like Pah and me in a way. There was no peace left in our world. Why was I fighting this? Maybe Alexio was right—nothing would make Pah happy. Was I simply afraid?

As I sat wondering what to do with myself, a small pair of arms encircled my neck. By the dirty nails and dark brown skin, it was easy to identify my sneaky visitor. "Good morning, Paimu. What have you been doing with yourself this morning?"

"Helping." She kissed my cheek and plunked down beside me. Her light brown dress was soiled and needed changing. I would have to wash it soon.

"Helping who? Tam the goat boy? You smell like a goat."

"Nobody cares what I smell like, Nefret. Why are you sitting here by yourself? Did you make Alexio angry?"

"My meeting has been delayed...have you been spying on me?"

She smiled, crinkling her wide nose. Paimu was a pretty girl, in an Algat sort of way. The Algat were generally friendly people but naturally suspicious and notorious for stealing whatever they wanted. My father said they would sell their children if they could get a good price for them. Algat loved nothing more than gold and silver. From what I remembered, Algat had high foreheads, wide noses and toothy smiles, but it had been six years since any of Paimu's people had visited our tribe. It was a strange thing indeed that some mother or father would leave a child behind.

She ignored my question and scooted up beside me. "Are you worried that Pah will beat you?"

"I don't know, Paimu." Attempting to change the subject, I asked her, "Where are Ziza and Amon?"

"Fighting with one another, as always." She offered me some of her grapes, and I accepted them from her sticky hand. "About you, of course."

I popped a grape in my mouth and frowned. "Me? Why are they fighting about me?"

"It's all foolishness. Who cares what they think?"

I could judge by her grown-up tone that she disapproved of their disagreement, which was more than likely about my sister and me. She tossed her last grape into the pool and laughed as the fish dove after it. Rinsing her hands in the cool water she said, "Can we go for a swim?"

"I cannot now; I am waiting to be summoned. But maybe later, little one."

With a sigh, she sat down beside me again and toyed with my silver earrings. Silver was rare in the desert. She touched them with her tiny fingers. "It's getting hot out. I think we should swim. Maybe if we swim deep enough we'll find some treasure in the water. Yes, we should find treasure!" She stood with a smile and tugged at my hand.

"Paimu, I told you I cannot. Please, come sit." She obeyed, but I could tell something troubled her. Finally she shared what was on her heart.

"Are you going to leave me, Nefret?" Her smile vanished, and distrust and anger flashed in her dark eyes. "I know you are—I had a dream."

"What are you talking about, Pai? I am not leaving." I shivered as a fleeting shadow passed behind her. It surprised me, but it was gone as quickly as it came.

"You will, and you will leave me behind. I will never see you again."

"What are you talking about?" Standing, I hugged her. She felt so frail and tiny, but she had the heart of a warrior.

"I had a dream about you—you and Pah. You left me, Nefret, and I never saw you again." She cried loudly, and the sound filled me with desperation.

"No, it was only a dream...hush now, little one. I will never leave you. I promise. Where I go, Paimu goes too." I cupped her face in my hand and stared her in the eye to show her I meant it.

Her lip quivered and she nodded. "You promise?"

"Yes, I promise."

She threw her arms around me again, hugged me once and then ran down the path that led to a nearby row of tents.

Pondering the meaning of her outburst, I was surprised by the arrival of a messenger. It was time to assemble for the meeting, time to hear what the Council had to say. I caught my breath and followed behind the tall, thin warrior. People gathered along the sides of the sandy path. Their smiling faces encouraged me; some even openly called me *anni-mekhma* as I passed by. I did not answer them or acknowledge the title—it would be inappropriate to do so with the trials having just begun, and I did not wish to court ill luck.

Pah arrived at the same time, also summoned back to the massive tent by a serious-faced messenger. We stood before the tent door, wondering who should enter first. I waved my hand to show deference to her as she stepped in front of me with her head held high. Walking behind her, my eyes widened at the sight of Father in his royal attire. He wore a tunic and pants of blue cloth; the tunic's neck dipped to the center of his chest to show an array of scars, chains and pendants, each representing something meaningful. The Meshwesh often memorialized special events with gifts of jewelry, and Father's display showed how much he was venerated by his tribe. His stone face revealed nothing, and with a wave of his hand, Pah and I obediently knelt before him. His brother Omel was to his left, and the tribal council surrounded them on either side. Farrah, the Old One, the oldest and most powerful member of the Council, sat to the king's right. She wore robes of white and gray, and her long, thick gray hair hung around her like a soft veil. Of all the faces that watched me, hers was the most intimidating. She spoke first, and her commanding voice filled the tent.

"Welcome, daughters of Semkah and Kadeema. You come before the Council today to declare your intentions to compete for the role of mekhma. Is this correct?"

Pah said calmly, "Yes, Farrah."

"Yes, Farrah," I replied less confidently.

"Very well, daughters." She paused and looked at each of us. "Know this…once you cast your incense into the smoke there is no turning back, no changing your mind. The smoke is a covenant with the tribe—you cannot call back smoke once it rises to the heavens. If it is truly your heart's desire to serve as mekhma, take the spoon in front of you and toss the incense into the flame. We will wait while you consider."

My mind ran through multiple scenarios, none of which I had the courage to pursue. Simply fleeing from the tent was not an option. How could I shame our father in such a way? I reached for a spoon, but not before Pah did. With unexpected quickness, she tossed the yellow incense into the fire, and the smell of ground herbs filled the tent. As her cloud faded, I held my breath, dug into the powder and tossed it into the flame. Our actions were met with an unexpected song from Mina.

She who gives her life for the tribes will always have life to give
Our mekhma is the blood of the clan, the heart, the life
Yield to her, enemies of the Meshwesh, for she is mighty!

When her song was complete she nodded to us and made the sign of respect, a raised upright palm. We acknowledged her with a nod, and Farrah continued.

"Today is both a happy day and a troubling one. Happy because we know that our clan will soon welcome a new leader, a woman to lead our people back to Zerzura, just as the prophecy foretold." The Council nodded their agreement and repeated the word "Zerzura" with reverence. "For some time the Council has considered your special circumstances and have sought the gods' help to discern the way forward."

I stared at her, the haze of the incense burning my eyes slightly. I tried to focus, to pay attention to every word as if my life hung upon her words. Truthfully, it did.

"I, Farrah, was there the night you were born, the night the falcon and the Bee-Eater flew into the birthing tent. From that day forward, we knew that you were not ordinary children—you had a special destiny. It has been many years since we had a mekhma to lead us, although your father has been an honorable king and has given his tribe much wealth through his wise dealings. His brother also has led his own tribe with wisdom and strength. We give thanks to them for keeping their tribes safe, but it is the Meshwesh way to serve queens rather than kings." Farrah paused so that the gathered leaders had the opportunity to agree with her. All did except for Omel, who merely stared at us, his face a mask. I was not the only one who noticed this. Father raised his hand to Farrah to prevent her from speaking further. His eyes flashed with anger as he brought the meeting to a halt waiting for Omel's acknowledgement.

Omel's face softened, but his eyes never changed. "That's the way it has always been," our uncle said finally. Satisfied that everyone was in agreement, Father relaxed and waited for Farrah to continue, but Omel had more to say. "But if we are going to adhere to the Old Ways, we must adhere to all of them. One cannot pick and choose which of the customs to follow. These things must be properly administrated or we risk again the wrath of the gods."

Father's deep voice bellowed, "What do you mean?" I watched the scene with wide eyes. I glanced at Pah, who was equally entranced. But like Omel, her face masked her emotions.

"Brother, my king, these are troubling times as you well know. We need a strong leader with undisputed authority. Our clan must not repeat the mistakes of the past."

Father seemed ready to thrash Omel, but Farrah's voice broke the tension. "Omel is correct, Semkah. The Old Ways must be followed."

"You can't ask me to do this."

"I haven't," Farrah said, drawing herself up, her back as rigid as her voice. Even sitting amongst the men who towered above her, she was a forbidding figure. *It was like magic, how she did that.*

"What is happening? What do they mean?" I whispered to Pah, but she ignored me. She sat perfectly still, her hands resting on her knees, palms down. Nobody answered me, although I knew they could hear me. Father's face said it all. Whatever custom our uncle referred to, it was not good. Would they require a life? My life? Would one of us have to die? My stomach twisted into knots. "What are these Old Ways you speak of, uncle?" I blurted out. "Tell us. We have a right to know."

Farrah answered for him, "It is Una and Uma we speak of."

Wracking my brain, I recalled scant portions of their story. It was never a tale I told around the fires at night, nor did anyone. This was only the second time I had heard the names spoken aloud. "What of them? Who were they?"

"Sisters they were, sisters who fought to lead the Meshwesh, and in doing so nearly destroyed the clan. Their hatred for one another was legendary—many families were left with no sons and daughters. From that day to this one, sisters have never ruled together in our clan."

Pah's voice sounded like cold steel. "One shall rule, one shall leave." Her voice sounded firm, deliberate. There was no surprise there.

"Leave?"

"Surely there must be another way," Father said.

"It must be *this* way. Omel is correct, Semkah."

Father's shoulders slumped and I whispered, "Father!" His eyes were tender as he gazed upon us. "Please," I pleaded with him.

"If it is the will of the clan, there is nothing I can do." His words hit my heart like well-placed arrows.

Desperation swelled inside me. Did everyone know this already? Was that what Alexio was trying to tell me? I stared into my twin's face, her green eyes averted, her face still a taut mask. "Pah, we can rule together, can't we? Tell them!" She did not answer me but kept her eyes focused on her hands. I saw nothing, not a tear, not a smile, nothing. Hopelessness swept over me.

Then the truth rose like the sun over the desert. She had known Omel's intentions all along. For Pah and our uncle, it was all or nothing.

Farrah spoke again, her voice softer, more patient but unyielding. "Even if you had the purest of intentions, Nefret, even if Pah did, it would not be enough. Ambitious men would always seek to divide you, and that would further divide the clan."

To Father she said, "Have you forgotten the bird, Semkah?"

"No, I haven't, and I remember that it died at your hands."

Farrah didn't flinch. "If you want them to live, it must be this way."

He did not answer. Wisely, his brother kept his peace while the Council agreed that these trials would follow the Old Ways.

I could do nothing to prevent it. Never had I felt so alone.

Chapter Four

The Trials—Nefret

"Now that you know what is at stake, perhaps you will take these trials more seriously. There will be three tests. You must pass all three, and the mekhma will win at least two. It is now that we ask your blood kin to leave us. No one shall influence the outcome of these trials." Without a question, our father, uncle and cousins left us with the six members of the Council and the two acolytes. I wanted to run after Father, but he offered me no solace; he did not meet my gaze or say a word to us. Even if I withdrew from the trials, it would do me no good. I had cast incense into the fire and released my soul to reach its destiny. Whether it would be here or somewhere else, I did not know.

"The mekhma is more than merely a queen. She is the keeper of the clan's stories—and its secret." It was Orba who spoke to us now. He was the youngest person on the Council and also generally the quietest. Small of frame with very little hair, he rarely appeared in public. "As our leader, you must know our stories, for they are a part of us. The mekhma is the keeper of stories. For this first trial, you will tell us a story. Who will go first?"

Pah spoke before me. "I shall go first. I am the oldest."

Farrah laughed at her. "How do you know this? I was there when you were born. Was it your head or your hand that emerged first from your mother's womb?" Pah looked confused. She had established herself as the oldest early in our childhood. I hadn't thought to argue with her.

Stunned into silence, Pah said nothing else. Orba spoke again, "Very well, Pah. You may go first." For the first time in our trials, Pah glanced at me, her head down, an unsure look upon her face. That was a rare thing to see, but it did not fill me with joy as I was sure it would have if the tables were turned. Was it true? Was I the oldest?

To everyone's surprise I said, "Please. I will go first, Orba."

With wide eyes the man looked at Farrah, who glanced about the tent. Nobody disagreed, and he gave his consent. Pah said nothing as I stood...

My mind raced—what story should I tell? The only one I could think of was the story of Zerzura. I took a deep breath and began.

"Hear me then, wise ones. Hear the story of Ma, the brave young man who, during the Times of Storms, led the people out of the dying desert to the abandoned White City of Zerzura.

"Once, the beautiful city had been home to the fair-skinned giants, the Nephal, but these giants had angered a powerful god. For crimes forgotten by men, the Nephal were cast out of Zerzura by the Unknown God after falling to his victorious arm in a great battle. The offended god cast them into a place beyond seeing. Ages would pass before another living thing walked on the streets of that city.

"For many seasons the Meshwesh endured the vicious sandstorms, the most ferocious the desert people had ever seen. The blasting red sands killed the livestock, destroyed the fruits and trees and stole the lives of many Treasures of the Tribe. Such a heartbreaking time has never since been known by our people.

"Desperate to find a place of refuge for the Meshwesh, Ma did the unthinkable; he stood before the white walls of Zerzura and prayed to the Unknown God. He begged the deity to allow him to take the city, to claim it for his own so his people would have shelter from the blasting sands. After he prayed, Ma looked up to see a Heret falcon watching him from the gate post. It observed Ma for a few minutes and then flew to take its spot atop the tallest tower in the city. All who had been reluctant to follow Ma now changed their minds—this was a sign! Ma led the Meshwesh into Zerzura and claimed it as his own.

I licked my lips and continued with my story.

"The Meshwesh rejoiced! They found refuge from the crushing sands and the relentless heat. Never again, they vowed. Never would they pack up their tents. Zerzura, the city nestled safely in the hills of the wilderness, would always be theirs. The giants who built the city had done so with skill—Ma knew the place would stand for a thousand years. Many fountains, patches of green grass and even orchards were contained within the city walls; there was more than enough to keep everyone happy. Many great houses stood empty, the beautiful artwork still perfectly painted on the walls. Scattered throughout the city and along the promenade were massive marble columns with intricate carvings. It was a rich place—even the bedchambers of the smaller homes were like lavish palaces to the Meshwesh. Ma and his warriors found an arsenal of weapons, some of which no man had ever laid eyes upon. He even found a great library, but many of the scrolls were written in a language he did not know.

"One such scroll had an unusual script that glowed in the moonlight. Ma and his wife, Sela, became obsessed with the scroll—they were convinced it would lead them to an undiscovered treasure.

"Some on the Council warned Ma and Sela against pursuing the knowledge of the scroll, but they would not heed this admonition. Ma called together the wisest members of his tribe and consulted the traders who came to visit Zerzura until he found one who could read the words. Finally they had their answer!

"'Beware the Lightning Gate! Moonlight opens the door, but a woman holds the key.'

"These were the words of the scroll. Ma trembled with fear at the warning, but his wife was intrigued. Some say that Sela had been enchanted by the scroll itself, that the words wove a spell around her heart. From that day forward, she no longer loved her husband or her tribe. The Council decided that the scroll referred to the western gate, which was flanked by unusual stones cut in the shape of lightning bolts. Every night the door would be shut, and no woman would be able to pass through the gate until sunup for fear of whatever door would be opened.

"For many years, nothing happened. All was well in Zerzura—it had truly become home to the Meshwesh, who thrived in the White City. Traders from around the desert came to see the great place. But in Sela's heart, all was not well. She had spent much of her time learning the language of the scroll. She found other scrolls to read until she spent every day in the library, forgetting her husband and children.

"One night, Ma's wife had a dream. A handsome man with pale skin and silver hair appeared to her. He rode the moonlight into her chambers and told her that her beauty had drawn him to her and that her knowledge of his language impressed him. Eventually, he revealed himself as the true king of Zerzura. He told her a woeful story of his wrongful imprisonment, of an unjust god, and how he deeply longed to walk through the White City, how he ached to hold her in his arms so she could become the true queen of Zerzura.

"Night after night the Moonbeam King, as Sela came to call him, visited her in dreams. He praised her beauty and confessed his love for her, even as Ma slept beside her. One night, the man told Sela how to set him free from his prison. She had to walk through the gate when the moon was full and whisper his name.

"The man told her his name, but he also commanded her to tell no one else. Revealing his secret name would mean death for her. Ecstatically, Sela hatched a plan. One night when the city was full of foreign traders, she would shed her queenly robes and breach the gate dressed as a man. Her handmaiden and confidante, Niri-ka, begged her mistress to change her mind. She reminded her that her husband loved her, but Sela was determined. Obediently, Niri-ka helped Sela slip out of her chambers, out of the palace and down to the courtyard. She passed easily through Zerzura to the Lightning Gate and made her way to the edge of the city. Nobody stopped her. Niri-ka watched in amazement as her mistress walked calmly past the guards. She watched when the queen passed through the gate, unveiled herself and called out the name of the Moonbeam King.

"Suddenly a powerful light shone on the other side of the Lightning Gate! It was so bright that it nearly blinded all the guards who kept the gate. Sela's garments flowed behind her as an evil wind began to blow into Zerzura. The man with the silver hair and pale skin walked toward the gate, and behind him were six giants of angry countenance. The silver man scooped up Sela as easily as he would a child and cut her throat with his sword before the guards could rescue her. She had been warned not to reveal his name, but she had not obeyed. In a panic, Niri-ka ran back to the palace to tell Ma what had happened. Ma and his warriors raced to the arsenal and charged to meet the unearthly foes. Ma fought bravely, but the giants overwhelmed the Meshwesh and killed many of the king's warriors.

"Niri-ka watched in horror. In the melee of swords and arrows, a tiny green Bee-Eater flew down and sat upon the Lightning Gate. It turned his head and stared at her. Despite her fear, she felt compelled to follow the bird. She walked through the scuffle, seemingly unseen. Giants and Meshwesh were all around her, but all she could see was the gate and the bird; it was always watching, coaxing her along. As she walked toward the gate, Niri-ka understood what she had to do. It was a woman who had released the Nephal, and it would be a woman who put them back into their prison. Niri-ka stepped through the gate. Her unfaithful mistress had told her the Moonbeam King's name, and now Niri-ka called to him, commanding him to leave Zerzura forever.

"The Moonbeam King and the giants dropped their weapons. They raged and cursed the Meshwesh but could not fight the invisible force that pulled them to the gate. The light once again blasted from the gate, and suddenly they were gone. Thanks to Niri-ka, the Meshwesh had been saved! Ma married Niri-ka, and the Meshwesh were happy once again."

I paused for a moment to catch my breath before continuing.

"Until many generations later…one night the Nephal poured through the Lightning Gate, and this time there was no woman's voice to send them back. No one knows who would have done such a thing—anyone who knew the name of the Moonbeam King was long dead. That night, giants stampeded through the city, shaking the ground as they ran, killing everyone in their path. They took back Zerzura with a white-hot rage. The Meshwesh fled the city and ran far into the desert. They watched the fires turn the White City black and listened with breaking hearts to the screams of the unlucky ones who had not escaped. The sounds of despair filled the night air. Onesu, their king, tried

to comfort his people even though his young wife Ze had not escaped.

"As they wept and watched, one of the wise women rose up amongst them and prophesied that one day a mekhma, a woman of strength and power, would take back the city and exact vengeance on the evil giants and their pale leader. So has been the hope of the clan for all these years." That was the end of the story, but passionately I added, *"One day, we will take back Zerzura, banish the giants and bring the Lightning Gate down so that never again will we lose our home."*

The Council had kept their silence the entire time, but now I could see the shimmers of tears in their eyes. They were moved, touched by the story—even Pah appeared transfixed. Nobody spoke, nobody moved. Only Mina smiled, and I took my seat beside my sister. The brazier in front of us sputtered, and the flame burned white.

Pah stood and began her story. She told the Story of the Bee-Eater and how it came to be the tribe's second symbol. I knew Pah hated storytelling. She would rather sulk than speak, but she told the story flawlessly, remembering to use her movements and facial expressions perfectly, as if she had told it a hundred times before. I listened respectfully and sat quietly even when she struggled to remember a point here or there.

When her story had ended, Pah returned to her kneeling position. The gathering did not cry as they had during my turn, but I could see they were impressed with Pah's retelling. They said as much as they complimented us on our recitations and our passion for the tribe's history.

"Now we must decide who won this trial. Let us pray to our ancestors to guide us." Obediently, we bowed our heads as Farrah entreated our foremothers and forefathers to guide their decision. When her pleas were completed, she gave instructions. "Pah, Nefret. Go now and stand by the doorway, one on either side. Hold out your hands, for each of us has a coin to give. Whichever daughter leaves with the most coins has won this trial. Whether you win or lose, save those coins. If you lose the trials you will need the coins for your journey. We will break our fast now but return this evening before the sun disappears into the sand."

We rose and did as we were told. My throat felt tired, and my thirst increased by the minute, but I held out my hands obediently. The Council members walked toward us, each holding a shiny gold coin in his or her hand. First in line was Farrah, her majestic gray and white robes hanging elegantly from her tall, thin body. She paused and looked at both of us before dropping her coin in my hand. I felt Pah's eyes upon me as all the Council members but one deposited their coins in my hands. Orba had decided against me and for Pah; I nodded politely as he left us. We were alone with only Mina and one other acolyte to attend us.

I clutched the coins in one hand. Feeling uncomfortable and hoping to make peace I said, "What if I were to give you these coins, Pah? Would it make a difference? What if I let you win? What would you say to that?"

Without warning, Pah slapped me. My skin radiated heat from the stinging strike, and my coins fell out of my hand. They made a dull sound as they fell on the thick carpet. Instinctively, I stepped back from her in case she struck me again. I had never been hit before, except on the practice field when we were children, learning the ways of the maiden warriors. Those strikes had not been deliberate, but this one was—and it struck right at my heart.

"I want nothing from you, Nefret! Nothing! Everything I have ever received has been at my own hands. I am not Father's favorite, nor do I hold Alexio's heart in my hand—I am not the tribe's treasure or the children's savior. I am Pah! I am the mekhma!" Her voice rang loudly in my ears. "I will *earn* my right to be called such. You cannot give that to me. It is not within your power! Queen's blood is in my veins too. Would you like to see it?"

Pah showed me her wrist and drew a small circular blade from her waist. My eyes widened, and I shook my head quickly.

"Are you sure?"

I shook my head over and over, clutching my face where she'd struck me. The shock of the assault had surprised me enough to stun me silent.

Mina did not speak, but she came to me and took my hand. She shook her head at Pah and defiantly stood between us. Pah snorted at me derisively and said, "I will win this, and you will leave. Save yourself some embarrassment if that is possible. Leave now, Nefret. I am telling you, you should leave now! If you do not, you will always regret it." I felt a slight shift in the air around us. It was as if in the otherworld, the words had been repeated, written down forever in eternity's library. With a wave of her hand she stormed out, leaving me gaping after her.

Mina picked up the coins and placed them in my hands, folding my fingers over them. She leaned forward, and I thought she would break her vow and speak to me. She had done so earlier when she sang for us; perhaps she was allowed to sing for us. I didn't know. Nevertheless, she did not speak to me now. She leaned her forehead against mine and hummed a haunting tune that I didn't remember but certainly felt as if I knew. It comforted me. She swayed to the sound of her song and gathered me into her arms. It reminded me of the mother I had never known. I laid my head on her shoulder. All of the fear, the grief, the uncertainty erupted into sobs. I cried until I could not cry anymore. When I was done, she took me by the hand and led me to the door. With a kind smile she left, and I walked out behind her.

"Nefret, your tent is this way." Alexio waited for me outside. I stumbled, making the coins jingle in my pocket as I walked behind him. I hoped no one stopped me—I wanted no one to see my sister's handprint on my face.

"Wait. Where are we going?"

"I am taking you to your new tent. Pah remains in your old one."

I had forgotten about that. For the first time in my life I would spend the night by myself. Thankfully, my friend did not interrogate me or scold me as he had earlier. The camp was quiet, much quieter than it had been just a short time ago. People moved out of the way as we walked through the short grass to my new home, for however long that might be. No matter what had happened today, I did not believe that I would win. In my heart of hearts, I truly did not. Pah was the better warrior, the bravest, the most determined. I could tell a good story and had some skill with a bow, but that was it. What was I thinking?

I did not linger outside the tent. I was anxious to be alone, away from the curious eyes of my people—and Alexio. "Thank you," I muttered as I slipped inside. My new tent was smaller than the one I had shared with my sister, but it was no less comfortable. Someone, no several someones, had been very busy making everything tidy for me. Suddenly, I remembered my treasure and ran to the neat pile of my personal belongings. Reaching for my mother's robe with shaking fingers, I untied the cord that I had bound it with. The necklace tumbled out of the sumptuous fabric and into my hands. Nobody had found it! I clutched it close; the metal felt cool and then warmed under my touch. So unusual, so rare. I couldn't help but wonder what treasure this was—perhaps it had magical powers. Adding my coins to the robe, I placed the necklace back inside and rolled it up again.

I collapsed on my cool blanket and rolled on my back, closing my eyes. Today seemed like a nightmare. If I tried hard enough, perhaps I would wake up. I rolled over on my side; my eyes felt heavy and soon I fell asleep.

I dreamed that I was in Zerzura. At least I thought it was Zerzura.

I wore white sandals and anklets of gold. I walked through the streets of the city, the walls white and shining bright in the morning sun. I heard the happy chants of my people saying, "Bless our mekhma! She is our treasure!" I felt a cascade of flower petals falling upon me as people tossed basketfuls of scented blooms down from structures high above me. I had never seen such a place! What walls! Surely giants had built these! The flowers tickled my face, and I brushed at them with my hand…I awoke in my own tent. Hanging above me, secreted in the cedar timbers that supported my tent, was a cluster of purple flowers. The petals had fallen onto my face as I slept.

Alexio! He must have hung them there when the tent was constructed. I smiled at the sight—what a thoughtful gift!

Someone must have visited me while I slept because a tray of bread, cheese, fruits and a pitcher of clear water waited for me on a nearby table. I ate hungrily, toying with the flower petals and daydreaming about life as Alexio's wife. It could never be; he was pledged to serve his tribe as husband to Farafra. I would serve my destiny in my own way, whether here or cast out in the sand sea. A lump rose in my throat as I devoured the warm, chewy bread and gulped down the water.

"It's time, Nefret. The trials continue." I looked up to see Alexio at the door of my tent.

"Have you heard? We will follow the Old Ways."

He nodded and strode toward me, his arms outstretched. I stood and fell into them. I didn't cry or make a sound. I clung to him like I was standing in quicksand and he was the only thing that could save me. We were so close; I could feel his heart beating through his tunic.

"You must win, Nefer-nefer." I smiled at hearing him use the name only he called me. "You have to win." Never had he hugged me so. In fact, we rarely touched, much less hugged. It was a bittersweet moment, to be so close to one destiny but commanded to seek another.

Alexio had been right all along. Pah was lost to me. I had to fight, not because I wanted my sister to lose but because I wanted to live. She had made it clear that she did not want any help from me. So be it. The gods would have their way after all, and there was nothing I could do about it.

Chapter Five

The Painted Stones—Nefret

I stepped away from Alexio, straightened my clothing and poured some water in a shallow bowl. I washed my face and patted it with a towel. "Are they all there?"

"Yes, all but you and your sister."

"Very well. Let's go." I ducked out of my tent and held my head high as we walked back through the crowd. Apparently, word that the loser would be banished had traveled around the camp. Even my children had gathered to see me. I smiled at them as they whispered, "Mekhma Nefret." No sense in playing coy now. I had won the first trial, and now I faced the second.

I wondered what the trial would be, but I did not bother to ask Alexio. He would not know, and I was not in the mood to speculate. As we approached the tent, the guards stepped out of the way and pulled back the flap for me. Alexio did not follow me in. Pah sat where she had sat before, her hands resting perfectly in her lap. I quickly sat beside her and faced the Council. I noticed that our father had not returned to the proceedings, which unsettled me.

Orba said, "Welcome back, daughters of Semkah. Let us proceed with our matter. Today you will show us your skills in intuition and strength. Before each of you is a row of stones." Mina removed the linen cloth to reveal the carefully arranged stones. There were seven in each row, each round and smooth. He continued, "There are times when a mekhma must rely upon her intuition alone. She should be strong and confident in her decision-making. She must also be able to speak to the gods to search out a matter and choose wisely. You have the same number of stones in front of you; each set has three stones with painted symbols on the bottoms. Each of you will take a turn uncovering the stones until one of you reveals all three of your symbols. You must prove the strength of your connection to the gods—and your intuition. Since Nefret went first the last time, Pah, you will go first now."

Looking confident, Pah nodded. She had changed her garments and unbound her hair; her long auburn tresses flowed behind her like a shimmering copper waterfall. She bowed down on the carpet, just as I had seen her do each night as she prayed to her many beloved deities. As she did so, I studied the rocks, looking for clues but seeing none. Finally Pah rose and selected a rock. She turned it over to reveal a red painted figure. She cast a sidelong glance at me, and I could see a smile curl on her lips.

How could I win this trial? I never prayed! Not to gods or ancestors; I sometimes talked to my mother, but she never spoke to me. I only worshiped when the tribe did. I had no connection to any god, nor would I pretend now that I did. It appeared as if my rebellious heart would cost me more than I could have imagined. Biting my lip, I stared at the stones and turned one over. Nothing. My heart sank.

My sister bowed herself to the ground again and entreated Hathor to guide her this time. She rose and selected another rock, which showed another red figure. Raising the rock over her head, she laughed. Apparently, the gods and goddesses were aligned against me. All eyes were on me as I stared at the stones. Looking at each one, I listened to my inner voice this time and finally decided on a stone. I guessed correctly, which surprised even me. I tossed the rock over and kept my focus on the remaining rocks.

Pah did not bow or beseech her deity aloud this time. She closed her eyes, and her upper body swayed slightly as if she were under some kind of spell or hearing music that no one else could hear. This continued for at least a full minute, but no one said anything to her. Stone-faced, the Council waited patiently for the anni-mekhma to make her decision. A cold shiver ran down my spine. Finally, with a dramatic nod of acknowledgement to some unseen voice, she reached for a rock and showed it to the Council. So confident was she that she did not even look—she flashed a joyous smile. When the Council did not applaud she turned the rock over to see for herself. The stone had nothing on it! Pah appeared confused and angry. She tossed the rock to the ground and glared at me as if I had something to do with her results.

My hand flew to my heart as the seriousness of the moment overwhelmed me. Calling upon my intuition, I studied the surfaces of the stones. Again, they gave me no clue. I reached for one but felt an unexpected disquiet rise in my spirit. No. Not that one. I touched the stone directly in front of me. No affirmation came, but no warning arose either. Holding my breath, I picked it up and turned it over to see my results. I did it! The Council politely gave their approval, and then their attention refocused on my sister.

Pah again began to pray and beseech Hathor for guidance. Less confident now, she ran her hands along the row of stones as if she could detect their undersides with just her palm. With a cool smile she touched a stone and flipped it over. Nothing! It was bare! Shocked, I turned my attention back to the stones. I did not pray aloud, but my mind pleaded for help.

I am Nefret, daughter of Kadeema and Semkah. If you ever loved me or cared for me, help me now...

Time seemed to slow as I stared at each stone. I reached for one and heard a small, still voice speak in my head.

No!

I drew my hand back with a gasp.

With shaking fingers I reached toward the next stone.

NO! I heard again, louder this time. I was surprised that no one else could hear the voice. Withdrawing my hand, I reached for the last stone in the row and heard nothing. Not a whisper. I picked it up and stared at the bottom. The sign of the Dancing Man was painted there, and I turned the stone around to show it to the Council. With loud trills and whistles, they celebrated. I won another round of the trials! Pah's face was like glass, hard and unmoving. I knew underneath her mask she fumed. I knew her too well to think otherwise, but the knowledge did not bring me joy.

"Come now." Farrah rose from the carpet and beckoned us to follow her. "Let us see who is the strongest. This trial is not over yet, Pah, Nefret. The tribe is waiting."

Without a word of congratulations or anything else, Pah stepped in front of me and followed Farrah and the Council out of the tent. I heard someone call, "Nefret has won the round!" I tried not to smile at our father, who lined the path with the other members of our tribe. Some shouted Pah's name, and others shouted mine, but our father looked sad. I had not thought much about it before, but Father would lose no matter who won. He was not an affectionate man, not as some fathers were, but at times he spoke kindly to us and often gave us gifts. Some of the older women said that when Kadeema disappeared, she took all of his love with her. I did not know what to believe. Pah had the idea that Father loved me more, but in that she was wrong. I was sure of it.

Now, Father looked more distressed than I ever remembered. One daughter would be cast out of the tribe—for the first time, I selfishly hoped it wasn't me. I kept my head down and followed behind Pah.

We stopped at the end of the camp. Someone had set up an array of short spears, and two bows with quivers full of arrows lay on the ground. I recognized my bow immediately, and seeing it made me more confident.

"Daughters of the tribe, Pah and Nefret. We thank you for your willingness to prove yourselves worthy to be mekhma. You honor us. Now, show us your strength!" The crowd cheered for us, and the Council clapped respectfully. Without an argument about who would go first, Pah walked to the edge of the prepared field and waved at the viewers. They clapped for her, women trilled and children chanted her name. Aitnu, the tribe's most prominent warrior, walked to her and gave her instructions. Alexio stood near me at the edge of the crowd. Our eyes did not meet, but his presence encouraged me.

Poised and confident, Pah picked up the short spear. Without much effort she adjusted her grip and walked back from the target. Like a dancer, she stepped and spun, sending the spear soundly to its mark. The gathering clapped in admiration, tambourines shook and music played. Pah's beautiful hair shimmered as she reached for another spear from the stand. Her lovely face revealed nothing, but I knew she was pleased with her performance. If I had not been her opponent, I would have cheered for her too.

This time, Pah walked further away from the target. The crowd whispered, and Aitnu appeared unhappy. My sister was obviously not following instructions. Even for Pah, this would be no easy shot. Again, she spun on her strong legs and lunged, sending the spear down the track. I watched the gleaming wood flash in the sun as it pierced the massive sandbag. More cheers for Pah erupted as she removed the last spear from the stand. She walked to the end of the path, which was marked with a bright flag. Playfully, she balanced the spear in her hand and walked back even further. She was showing off, showing our tribe that she was the stronger sister, the braver one, the more daring of the two of us. I could have told her she need not have worried. Everyone already knew that Pah was stronger than me. The crowd whispered; I could not hear what they said, but I knew they were impressed.

She spun about, stepped twice and threw her body forward, sending the spear toward its intended mark. The spear arced and sailed through the air, falling a few feet in front of the target. She missed! Nobody clapped, but I had no illusions about what happened. I glanced at Alexio. He gave me a resolute stare, and I got the message.

"Nicely done, sister," I said as she passed me.

"Good luck to you, Nefret," she purred proudly. I waited as the son of Aitnu retrieved the thrown spears and returned them to their stand.

My palms were sweaty as soon as I picked up the spear. It was not my weapon of choice, and it felt heavy and clunky in my hand. Nevertheless, I walked to the marker and stood staring at the target, which seemed to rest on the other side of the desert. Gripping the weapon, I ran back and then forward two steps, arched my back and released the spear into the sky. It whizzed to the target and hit it near the bottom. My throwing technique was not as efficient as Pah's, and I had no dancing skills, but I could do this. If I stayed focused and didn't attempt fancy shots as my sister had, I could at least finish without shaming our father.

Tambourines shook, and some of my tribe supported me with cheers and applause. Especially vocal were my children, led by Paimu. With a sigh of relief, I picked up the second spear and walked back to the throwing line. I spoke to that inner voice again: *Help me!* I heard nothing and decided that what I had heard earlier was my own imagination. The setting sun cast vivid colors on the horizon, and time slipped by as I gauged the target again. I stepped back, then forward, arched my back and threw. I gasped as the spear blew past the target and landed with a thud in the sand. The crowd grew quiet, and I did not wait for their applause for none would be coming. With the last spear in my hand, I walked back to the line. I tucked a wayward strand of hair behind my ear, stepped back, then forward using the strength of my whole body to launch the spear this time. This time the spear landed in the center of the sandbag, and my tribe cheered with excitement. I tried not to look but stole another glance at Alexio, who smiled at me. I noticed that Aitnu hung close by my sister and whispered to her as she watched me. She nodded her head and frowned.

Farrah announced, "This round has ended in a tie!" She clapped, her colorful bracelets rattling. She raised her hands, encouraging the crowd to cheer loudly for the anni-mekhmas. "Now we shall watch as the daughters of Semkah show us the power of their bows!" More applause erupted from the gathering as my sister and I took our spots on the line.

"Do you think you have a chance at beating me?" Pah taunted me quietly as we stood side by side strapping on our quivers. I nocked an arrow, released it and watched it zip to the sandbag.

"Yes, I do. You are a show-off, Pah. You make mistakes."

She hissed at me and followed my arrow with one of her own. There were seven arrows in each of our quivers; for each pull of my bow, Pah matched me perfectly. No arrows missed. No arrows fell short. When the first round was spent, Aitnu instructed us to walk back and refire our refreshed arsenal. It would make the trial more challenging, but I felt confident that I could manage the distance. My arms began to burn a little as I took shot after shot at the sandbags. Pah and I did not miss a shot.

"It is clear that the daughters of Semkah are both strong women," Farrah said to the crowd. "But now we shall see another demonstration. Aitnu, prepare to release the birds. Now, Pah and Nefret, show us again your skill with the bow. The first to strike the bird with an arrow will win this round."

Pah's face crumpled. She cared nothing for children and had even less care for adults, but birds she loved with all her being. How many wounded birds had she healed, with help from Father? Even now she had a cage of tiny songbirds in her tent. At times it seemed as if she spoke their language. Aitnu's son handed us a fresh batch of arrows. These were longer, with shorter tufts of feathers that would help the arrow scurry along to its intended victim. My arrows had bright red feathers and Pah's were blue, presumably to help the Council determine who delivered the winning shot if there was any question. I hoped that if I was lucky enough to strike a bird it would die quickly and not suffer.

Two men carried a rattan basket of birds to the sandbags. We nocked our arrows and raised our bows to the sky waiting for the birds' release. Aitnu watched us and gave the signal to the men, who then released the birds. I shot first, and the arrow narrowly missed a darting wren. Darkness encroached on the tournament, so I quickly lined up another shot as Pah took hers. With precision her arrow whizzed through the air and struck a less fortunate wren, which immediately tumbled to the ground. Today's contest had finally ended with Pah as the victor.

The tribe applauded and cheered for Pah, and her sadness quickly disappeared. I stepped out of the way as the people clamored around her. Some were polite enough to congratulate me as well, but it was Pah's performance that most impressed them. I left the crowd behind hoping to find some food and somewhere to think about what had happened and what would come next.

"Nefret! Wait," Father called to me. Tired and sweaty, I did as he asked.

"You did well. You should be proud of your performance—I am." He put his hand on my shoulder and looked me right in the eyes.

"Thank you, Father," I murmured. He hugged me, which was a strange experience. Savoring the moment, I closed my eyes and clutched my quiver and bow. When I opened my eyes, I saw Pah staring at me from the center of the cheering crowd, her green eyes flashing angrily. Before I could say her name she stormed away, a retinue of young men and women clustered around her. I sighed and our father grasped my arms gently.

"We will talk tomorrow. I must go find your sister now. Rest well, for tomorrow's trial will require all your skill and strength. That is all I can tell you."

"Thank you, Father. I will." We parted ways, and I walked back to my tent with Paimu dashing to my side.

"Princess, you almost won. I cheered for you! But it is no matter, for you won the other challenges. Just one more now!"

I smiled down at her. "Yes, just one more." She hugged my leg and raced away. "Where are you off to now?" I called after her.

"I am going to get my things."

"Why? Where are you going?"

"With you! I am moving in to your tent now."

I laughed. "Of course you are. Go get your things." Her beautiful smile spread across her face, showing her missing front tooth and otherwise perfectly white teeth.

This could be my last night with my tribe. I should spend it with someone who loves me.

Chapter Six

Treasures of the Tribe—Nefret

The Council dispatched a guard to stand at the door of my tent. My guard, a young man named Essa, surprised me by calling me outside. With a confident, over-friendly smile, he let me know that he had been sent for my security. I could not discern if there was some unknown threat that warranted such an action or if he was meant to keep me from running away, but I didn't ask him any questions.

Awareness crept over me. Now I clearly knew that I wanted to be mekhma, to serve my people, to protect Paimu, to lead us all back to Zerzura and take back what was ours. I did not discern the exact moment that this occurred, but my heart had indeed changed.

Singing to myself, I removed my tunic and washed my body with the scented water Farrah had so graciously provided for me. It had been a kind gesture, and I half wondered if Pah was being treated so royally. I had a lavish buffet of the tribe's best food on my cedar table, and my pitcher was full of sweet pomegranate wine—a truly thoughtful gift. The servant who had brought them was not a man I recognized, but I accepted them graciously. I was dressing for bed and thinking of pouring some wine when a scream outside my tent startled me out of my song. I ran to the sound, the voice of a young girl—Paimu! Essa had restrained her, holding her by her skinny arms and laughing at her as she struggled against him. I wanted to slap him in his pretty face.

"Let me go! Let me go! Nefret!"

"Stop that! Essa—what do you think you are doing? Turn her loose!"

Essa laughed, and his shoulder-length dark hair half hid his perfect nose and wide, dark eyes. "If I do, she may bite me, anni- mekhma."

"Nonsense. Let her go now. I command it."

He released her and lifted his hands in a gesture of surrender. Paimu kicked his shin, and he laughed again as he hobbled away from her. "She can't be here, anni-mekhma! The Council has given strict orders that both you and your sister are not to be disturbed or have any visitors. You should rest because tomorrow's trial will be grueling."

Paimu pushed past him and into my tent. He reached for her, but I stepped in his way, unaware that my bare shoulder was showing. He stared at it as if he had never seen a bare shoulder before. Maybe he hadn't. Suddenly, I blushed and covered my shoulder with the loose robe.

"Paimu is my guest. I have taken care of her all her life. I am not going to abandon her tonight just because the Council wants to keep me away from everyone. She has no one but me."

"I only want to be obedient to the Council—and to serve you, Nefret." He stepped toward me. He towered over me by at least a foot and a half. Essa had a fine, strong body, as far as I could tell, and I could see his face had softened as he looked into mine. No woman could deny that Essa was the most beautiful man in the Meshwesh or any other Red Lands clan—even Alexio paled in comparison to him for physical beauty. In a whisper he said, "What if I could arrange for us to be alone later? Would that interest you? You are a beautiful woman, Nefret, and I find you…" He lifted a strand of hair from my face and touched my cheek briefly. "I watched you every day and hoped you would see me. Am I not appealing to you?"

"I think the heat has gone to your brain, Essa." I stepped away from his friendly hands and seductive eyes. "Go take a few draughts of water to clear your head." I stepped backward and nearly tripped. It was dangerous being too close to him, under the stars, with my skin perfumed with exotic scents.

Suddenly the truth occurred to me. *This was a test! A test set by Farrah! She seeks to prove my virtue!*

I smiled and stepped back again. "I am going inside my tent now with Paimu. If the Old One wants to speak to me, I will be here. Please do not come in unless I ask you to. Thank you, Essa."

I walked inside and found Paimu still whimpering about her arm. She reached for the wine, but I forbade her to drink it. What if it had a love potion in it? I took the pitcher outside and poured it in the sand right in front of Essa. I wanted him to know that I knew what he was up to. The Council would test me, would they? Well, let them! I would not fail this particular test. I shook out the last drops of the wine and stared at the mess it left behind. It looked like blood poured out on the sand.

"What are you doing?" Essa demanded. His seductive attitude had vanished like smoke in the wind.

Farrah, whose tent was only a few feet away from me, walked outside, her scarf covering her head. It was common knowledge that she spent her evenings wandering the desert looking for signs and portents. I supposed she was headed out for just such a walk now. She stared at the red sand and then at me. Essa walked away, embarrassed, but Farrah smiled as if to say, "Ah, you passed the test." With a nod and a quick scan of the heavens, the old woman walked down the path and out of the camp. If I followed her, what I would see?

I snickered thinking of how Pah might have done with her test, if she'd had a similar one. I wondered who they would send to tempt her. *Oh no! Alexio! Please, my ancestors, do not let it be Alexio! He is not for her!*

I walked back inside and found that Paimu had made her bed right beside mine. I recognized the familiar sapphire silk blanket I had given her, some of my old tunics from when I was a child and the soft white leather sandals a friend of mine had made for Paimu. Reaching for my hairbrush, I cajoled her into letting me brush her hair. She complied and even allowed me to make a small braid and cinch it with a piece of white leather. She looked one hundred percent better, and I told her so. Handing her the dull mirror, she gave herself a gap-toothed smile.

"Eat, Paimu, and then we will go to bed. Have you washed your hands and feet?"

"No, but I am not dirty."

I popped her bottom playfully. "Let us see them. Oh my." I pretended to be shocked. "Those are so dirty, we could plant flowers with them. Let's wash the sand away, if you don't mind."

She giggled and allowed me to help her. She could do it all herself, but what if this was indeed the last time that I would be able to do such a thing? How was I ever going to leave her? My own heart? I loved Paimu—she was the little sister I never had. Perhaps that was why Pah hated her so much. Who knew?

Pah is lost to you, Nefret.

I could hear Alexio's voice ringing in my ear. Alexio! I would have to see him, somehow. Essa had stormed off, but knowing Farrah she would have him back here in a few minutes, if nothing else to save face and demand that he actually "protect" me from whatever dangers she imagined I faced.

After her bird bath, Paimu talked animatedly about the contest and how she could climb a tree now without any help. "When all this is over, you can show me again." She nibbled on the chula bread, dipping it in olive oil and pepper sauce before gobbling it up. Once she finished off the chula, she devoured the olives and the dates. I thought she would be sick if she didn't slow down and told her as much. "Oh, I never get sick. Never. One time I ate an entire pat of goat cheese without anyone to help me. I did not get sick at all."

"Don't you miss staying with Ziza?"

"Ziza has her sister, and I have you."

"Yes, but it's only one night, little one. I don't know what tomorrow may bring. If anything were to happen to me, return to Ziza's family. Her mother loves you."

At long last, Paimu stopped eating. Her wide eyes were full of tears. "You cannot go! Please do not leave me. I will have no one if I do not have you." Her smile disappeared, and her face contorted into a sob.

"Paimu, you must be brave. I have to make myself be brave, believe me, but I am trying. You try too. Be my sister, be my brave sister. No matter what the gods have ordained for us, we will meet it bravely and with kindness to others." I held my arms out to her, and she cried on my shoulder. I scooped her up and carried her to the bed. We lay down together and I held her while she cried herself to sleep.

Silent tears slid down my face too. Some tears were for Pah, my first friend and twin sister. I cried for the sweet girl I knew, the one that was hidden under layers of bitterness and imagined offense. I cried for our childhood that had been far too brief, and then I cried because one of us would leave and we would never see each other again. Then my tears were for Paimu. Eventually the tears subsided and I covered Paimu with the thick quilt, and soon I was sleepy too. I hadn't meant to cry; now I felt empty, tired. As I closed my eyes, within seconds I traveled to the dream world…

My heart pounded and my bare feet stomped on the cool stones as I ran through a narrow entrance inside a series of stone walls. Someone ran behind me, but I dared not look back. Up ahead I saw a flicker of flame; the light pierced the darkness and beckoned me to safety. My image and that of my husband mocked me from the painted walls that surrounded me. My long hair streamed behind me, and I felt naked in the thin white gown I wore. Gold cuffs were at my wrists and a heavy necklace thumped on my chest as I bolted toward the light. The sound of sliding stone came from behind me, and a thunderous shake followed. Trapped! I am trapped! I spun about to see a small child, a boy with red hair and dark eyes, reaching for me. I grabbed his hand and we continued to run with all our might to the light ahead of us.

Almost there…Run, Smenkhkare!

We turned the corner. The light was just a few feet away and moving…

I awoke with a start, immediately aware that someone else was in the tent with Paimu and me. She slept peacefully beside me, unaware of my terror and overwhelming anxiety. I peered into the darkness, wondering if perhaps an assassin had come to take my life. It had been several years since our camp had been raided by cutthroats, but it had happened many times in the past. I slid my hand under my pillow and felt for the small blade I kept there. In a panic, I remembered that I had taken no such preparations in my new tent. I sat up slowly, peering into the black.

A flicker of light appeared in the corner of the room. It bounced and expanded until it was the size of a man's fist. My breath caught in my chest as I froze, mesmerized by the sight. The light flickered again and expanded to the size of my shield, which lay on the other side of the tent along with my arrows and bow. Suddenly, the light blast brightly, so much so that I had to shield my eyes with my hands.

Fear washed over me and I fell to the ground on my face, unable to look at the increasing light. I remained in that position for an unknown length of time.

I heard a warm voice say, *"Do not be afraid."* At his words, the uncontrollable fear lifted, and I cautiously raised my eyes. A man wrapped in white fire hovered in the corner of my tent, his face obscured by the radiance. The light pulsed once and then dimmed, but his face remained hidden in the moving light.

"My lord, who are you? Why are you here?"

"I am known by many names, but none that you would know." The light decreased in brilliance, but I still could not see his face. *"I would make myself known to you."*

"I do not understand."

"Peace, daughter of the Red Lands. You will understand. It is I who leads you. Even now I lead, but will you follow? Even when you cannot see the way? Will you trust me even when you cannot see me? When all others turn against you?"

"Yes, lord. I will."

I had no idea what I had promised this Shining Man, but I knew I must obey. His light swirled about me, filling me with joy like I had never experienced. For one brief moment, love surrounded me and my soul leaped. No words passed between us, but knowledge flowed into me. Knowledge I promptly forgot.

He knew all about me, and somehow I realized that I knew him. He accepted me, welcomed me, called me to him. I caught my breath—how wonderful to be known by such a one! Then in a blast of light the Shining Man vanished, taking all his delightful, unearthly love with him.

With a heart full of peace, I fell into a deep slumber.

Chapter Seven

The Accusation—Nefret

I awoke to the sound of shouting. Paimu was gone, probably off to see her friends Ziza and Amon. I rubbed my eyes. Feeling tired from my night's encounter, I had no time to consider all that had happened. The Council would expect me to appear in my father's tent ready to perform the last trial, but from the sounds of stirring in the camp I needed to move quickly.

"Pah! Pah! Pah!"

I walked to the tent flap and watched as people streamed by me. Forgetting my knotted hair and crumpled clothing, I followed them, curious to see what was happening.

"Powerful with a spear—of great courage and strength! Pah should be our mekhma! Who is with me?"

One of my sister's friends, Ayn, stood beside Pah, holding her hand in the air; it was the sign of victory. Some of the crowd cheered and applauded; others murmured and pointed at the show Ayn was making. One of the children noticed me and shouted my name. This silenced the crowd, and their attention turned to me.

"This is her sister. Isn't she anni-mekhma too? Have the trials ended?" they asked one another. Ayn ignored both their questions and my presence. Paimu found me and clung to my leg fearfully. Ayn walked in a circle, holding Pah's hand high with one hand and one of Pah's spears with the other. She continued with her rant.

"Can anyone compare to Pah? Offer your pledge now and greet our new mekhma!"

"What is this?" Farrah entered the circle and challenged Ayn. "What are you doing?"

The tall young woman dropped Pah's arm and raised a defiant chin to Farrah.

"I am showing my support for Pah—the true choice for mekhma!" A few of the young women cheered at the acclamation until they fell under Farrah's watchful eye. The only sound heard then was the sound of banners flapping in the breeze and the distant sound of a goatherd's lute.

"Foolish girl! Do you think you can sway the Council or the people with this unseemly show? What is the meaning of this?"

Ayn did not back down, although I noticed that Pah had wisely cast her eyes to the ground, avoiding Farrah's piercing gaze. "I meant no disrespect, Old One, to you or the Council. However, is there a rule that says I cannot recommend my friend? That I cannot testify to her commitment and integrity?"

"What are you suggesting, Ayn?" Alexio stepped out of the crowd and stood beside me.

Farrah waved at him, warning him to be silent. "Speak plainly now, girl," she said to Ayn.

Ayn raised her head higher and returned Farrah's bitter stare. "Very well. Isn't it true that an anni-mekhma must be prepared to yield her soul, mind and body for the good of the clan?" Here she paused. "And that her maidenhood must be intact?"

"You know that it is true. What is your point?"

I stiffened—a feeling of dread rose up from within me.

"How can you be sure that Nefret has not yielded her body? I know Pah has always acted virtuously, but how can we vouch for someone whose heart has so obviously been given?"

My face reddened as the whispers circulated around me. "That is a lie!" I yelled. "I have yielded nothing!" Even as I said the words, I knew in my heart that it was not entirely true. I had not given my body to Alexio, nor had he asked me to, but my heart...that was another story.

"Have a care for your words, girl! These are serious charges." She lowered her voice and circled Ayn like a hawk stalking a snake. "Is this a charge you bring too, anni-mekhma Pah, or is this merely camp gossip?"

Pah swayed nervously and shook her head. "I do not accuse my sister." I breathed a sigh of relief but she added, "However, I do not condemn those who have doubts about either of us. I only want what is best for the people."

"Very well." Farrah drew herself tall and straight. "Let us settle this matter now. Follow me to my tent, anni-mekhmas. We will know who is intact and who is not."

Farrah stormed through the camp, and the people shuffled to get out of the way. I walked behind the older woman with my head held high. For once I was not going to let Pah step in front of me. How dare she accuse me of such a thing! She knew perfectly well I had not given away my maidenhood! I had no idea what test I would now be forced to undergo, but I would have to endure it. On this I was in the right. Mostly.

I stepped inside Farrah's tent and explored the contents with my eyes. It had been many years since I entered her abode; I had been small enough to perch on her ebony and enamel stool then. I used to trace its ornamental pictures of cavorting animals with my fingers. How delightful to see those animals there again, but how sad was this moment. My mind was filled with memories of Farrah exhorting me, "Look into the fire. Tell me what you see." I never saw anything, and eventually the Old One stopped inviting me to look or to visit.

Now the same gold medallions hung from the tapestried walls, new birds chirped noisily in their silver cages and the aroma of exotic scents again overwhelmed my senses. It was as if nothing had changed. Except I was no longer that child and the Old One looked truly old now.

"Sit. Both of you. Mina, prepare for the examination." Surprised, I glanced behind me. As quiet as a sand mouse, Mina had slipped in unnoticed, except by Farrah. She scurried away to attend to her task, and I sat facing my sister and the Council's head. "There can be no question about your qualifications. I want you to tell the truth now. Have you, Nefret, lain with a man?"

"No, I have not." I met her gaze squarely.

"Have you made any promises or pledges to anyone?"

"No, I have not. I would have thought you knew this, since you sent Essa to my tent last night."

"I sent no one. What are you talking about?"

Shocked, I said in a rush, "Essa came to my tent and said that the Council had sent him to watch over me. Is this not true?"

"I sent no one and know nothing about this. Perhaps your sister can enlighten me."

"Me? I know nothing, Farrah. Why ask me?" Her eyes flashed in anger, but behind them shifted something. Amusement? Her voice lacked sincerity.

Farrah grunted and pulled something from her pocket and tossed it in the flame of a nearby candle. The flame sparked, turned blue and returned to its low burn. "Your words do not fill me with confidence, Pah."

Pah's dark green eyes were like two steady fires burning back to Farrah. "I know nothing."

"Very well. As your friend has raised doubts about your sister's maidenhood, I am forced to confirm it. Still it would be unfair for her to endure this humiliation alone. You too will be examined, and my findings will be shared with your father, the Council and in fact all the Meshwesh."

I blushed but we both agreed, and Farrah's tone softened. "We must show the people that the mekhma is in control of her heart." She sighed and added, "If your uncle had not insisted in following the Old Ways, this would not have been necessary. Now we must do all things with care. Nefret, follow me."

I did as I was told. Pah turned her back respectfully as Farrah lifted my tunic and I endured her uncomfortable probing. It was quick yet humiliating, just as she predicted. "No, you are intact. Now Pah."

As my sister did for me, I turned my back as Farrah repeated the physical examination and declared her also intact. "All this fuss for nothing! Do you see? A few words can change a life! It can change your destiny. Have a care, anni-mekhmas, for what you allow to be done in your name." Farrah washed her hands and rubbed them with oils. "Now, Nefret, comes your first test of leadership."

"What do you mean?" Pah blurted out, her offense obvious. I imagined her thoughts: *Why does Nefret get chosen for a test and not me?*

"An accusation was made against Nefret. It has been proven a lie. As anni-mekhma, she must address the lie and deal with the offender. Unfortunately, you do not have much time. The final trial begins after breakfast."

Pah gasped in surprise. "What? What do you mean deal with the offender?" Ayn was and had always been her closest friend. I had no doubt that my sister had encouraged Ayn's outburst, but as always, she did not think things through. My sister may have had all the courage, but she had not much in the way of wisdom.

"Yes, it is her right. She may claim the girl's property—she may have her beaten by her mother or she may make a public spectacle of her and parade her about the camp on a rope if she likes. It is no concern of yours, unless you have something to say."

Pah stared at the carpet and shook her head.

"Speaking lies or repeating them about an anni-mekhma is as serious a charge as speaking against the mekhma. It will not be allowed, nor will the people allow it to go unpunished."

"Nefret, you cannot do this," Pah said, rising to her feet. "She has done nothing but repeat what she heard. It is no secret that you desire Alexio! How can you deny it?"

It was my turn to rise now. "You would come to Ayn's defense but would leave me to face an angry crowd? You have no right to ask me anything! It is you who pines for Alexio! It is you who sent Essa to my tent! Go ahead! Deny it!"

"I deny nothing!" she said, her eyes like lightning glass again, her mouth a firm pair of pink lines.

Farrah laughed sourly. "And you wanted to serve together? Now do you see why this is not possible? Make a decision, Nefret. We must go outside now, and I will tell the Meshwesh the truth."

Farrah rose from the carpet with Mina's help. She walked out to face the curious crowd, and again we trailed behind her. I was surprised to see my father standing outside with his king's robes on and ready to pass judgment if called to do so.

Farrah did not stop to speak with him, and neither did we. The gathering moved to the edge of camp, to the site where Ayn had made her accusations against me. My mind ran wildly; what would I say? I had no idea. I stood beside Farrah with my head held high, hoping that inspiration would come quickly.

"Words were spoken here this morning. Serious words." The crowd murmured their agreement and surrounded us in a loose circle. "I have examined our anni-mekhmas and found these words to be false." The people expressed their shock and disapproval with hisses.

All eyes were on me as Farrah continued, "Where is the accuser?" Hands shoved Ayn into the circle. As she stood before me I could tell by her demeanor that she was unrepentant yet a little less confident now. I knew that I should not, but I felt sympathy for her; Ayn was another victim of Pah's incessant scheming.

I wondered what prize she had been promised for perjuring herself. For her sake, I hoped it was worth it. Ayn's family hovered at the edge of the crowd, her mother's face the picture of fear and worry.

Farrah faced the girl. "Ayn, you have brought dishonor upon yourself and your family today with your false accusations. Look at your mother's face! See your father Nari's shame! Now, we shall hear from the one you slandered. It is Nefret's right to demand retribution. What say you, anni-mekhma?"

The morning air felt stagnant; any breeze blowing had disappeared. The eyes of the tribe watched anxiously, and even my father seemed uneasy about my decision. If I condemned Ayn, the tribe would fear me and Farrah would approve, but if I showed her mercy, the family would thank me and my children would approve. I had no way of knowing what Father would recommend. I had seen him sentence a man to die and in the same afternoon, forgive another. What would Pah do if she were in my place? I cast those questions aside. If I was going to rule, I would have to follow my own conscience.

"Daughter of the tribe, I bear you no ill will. I know that until this day you have not been a malcontent, nor have you brought shame on your family. Is this not true, my people?"

The Meshwesh agreed with me. Indeed, until this day, Ayn had done nothing but serve the tribe as an honorable and worthy person. "Therefore, I am inclined to believe that you did not conceive this deception yourself but were under the influence of others." The crowd gasped at my words, and I could see my father shuffling amongst them. Ayn dropped her face to the sand and stared at her sandals. That was all the proof I needed. Tellingly, Pah had not flinched or showed any response to my veiled accusation. I expected nothing less, yet it angered me that she who had begged for her friend's life in private would not lift a hand to save it now. I had no doubt Pah's whispers had ignited this flame.

When Ayn did not answer I pushed her harder. Stepping close to her I said in a loud whisper, "You said yourself that others told you this lie about me. Am I not to know who these others were, Ayn?" Still she offered no answer. Ayn's mother, Namari, began to cry softly; her husband tapped her shoulder to remind her to appear strong.

With a firm resolve, I stepped back and said, "Mother and father of Ayn, come speak to your daughter now before I pass judgment. Remind her that it is better to tell the truth than to spread a lie." Namari ran to Ayn's side and grasped her hand. Her father did not stir but stood firm, glancing ashamedly at his king.

Although Namari spoke in low tones, I heard her plead with her daughter, "Speak the truth and all will be well, Ayn!" Ayn shook her head, staring at the ground and refusing to speak or acknowledge Namari's pleas. Paimu lingered nearby, but I gestured for her to stay back.

"Very well, Ayn. You leave me no choice. As Nefret, I forgive you for your hasty words…" Ayn lifted her surprised face to me. Whatever she had expected, it had not been this. But I wasn't through. "However, as anni-mekhma, I must demand repayment for your offense against me. Do you now confess that you were wrong in accusing me?" I stood in front of her. We were so close, I could hear her breathing.

"I do so confess it. I was wrong." The older girl's voice broke, and she could see that Pah, her dearest friend, had not laid a finger on me to prevent me from punishing her. Her round, brown face crumpled like a flower crushed beneath the weight of a heavy foot. Still, Pah said nothing. She looked bored with the proceedings, unconcerned with the fate of her friend although she had begged for leniency just a few minutes ago. Pah was nothing if not changeable. To some her unwillingness to defend the outspoken Ayn meant very little, but Pah's silence surprised the friends who had prematurely acclaimed her as their mekhma. No one would trust her now.

"I claim all your silver, Ayn hap Nari." Ayn's face fell, but the girl offered no complaint. "And there is one more thing…I command you to care for Paimu if something should happen to me. You will love her and take care of her like she was your own sister, no matter what happens. Do you understand?" Ayn raised her curly head, her dark brown eyes meeting mine.

"You honor us, anni-mekhma," Namari said in a relieved voice. Ignoring the whispers of the people who gathered around us, I completed my judgment with a pronounced nod of my head as I had seen Farrah do a hundred times before. No doubt many would express disappointment that I had not sought greater retribution, as my sister or Farrah would have done.

"Gladly, anni-mekhma Nefret. I will do this."

"NO! I will stay with Nefret! Let me go, Alexio!" I ignored the child and whispered in Ayn's ear. "Be a better sister to her than Pah has been to me. Do you have sisters, Ayn?"

"No," she whispered back.

"Now, you do."

To my utter surprise and shock, she fell to her knee and raised her palms to me in the sign of respect. She was offering me her fealty and friendship! I waved my hands over her to show her I accepted her. She rose with a relieved look on her face. Looking to my left, she stared at Pah, who still seemed unmoved. Suddenly Ayn spat on the ground near Pah's feet and went to speak to Paimu. The little girl was still combative and ready to fight for her chance to stay with me.

I called to her, "Go now, Paimu. I must begin my next trial. I shall come see you in Ayn's tent when I am finished. Be a good girl." She relented and followed after Ayn, who tried to engage her in small talk. Pah drifted off into the crowd, no doubt to reinvigorate her supporters. Or try to.

Farrah smiled at me, showing perfectly white teeth. "Child, you are full of surprises. A reasonable and thoughtful judgment. You will make a great mekhma. But tell me, who provides you with such good counsel? I see that Pah has her supporters. Where are yours? Your father, perhaps?"

"No, I have no supporters. Except Paimu and the other children. It just came to me." Thoughtfully I added, "I guess the Shining Man is leading me."

"Who is this Shining Man you speak of? An Egyptian god, perhaps? Amun?" Farrah's eyes peered into mine, looking for an answer to a question she had not asked yet.

"No. He is not an Egyptian god, at least I do not think so… but I have seen him."

Farrah clucked her tongue and shook her head, mumbling under her breath. "No Isis or shining god for me. I prefer to pray to my ancestors or to Ma'at. They have seen us this far, and they can carry me back to Zerzura."

She spun about in her grey and white robe, her hair a beautiful mass of curls that trailed down her back. Words came to my mind, words I did not speak aloud.

No, you shall not go to Zerzura, Old One. Your time here comes to an end.

I shivered as the words drifted away and Farrah paused on the path still speaking to me. I saw her mouth and focused my mind on understanding what she said.

"Come, come, now. Let us go! Orba and your father will be waiting!"

Chapter Eight

The Final Trial—Nefret

For this trial, the tent was full of people. Pah and I were invited to sit on the tiger furs before our father's seat. We faced the people, who smiled and offered us well wishes. Nobody spoke about what might happen, about how either Pah or I would be banished to the Red Sands if not chosen. How morbid! If only we could have found a way to defy the prophecy and rule together.

Ah, but Pah would never allow such a thing to happen. I knew that now, even if I had not believed it before. Feeling sentimental for a moment, I slid my hand under hers and sighed as she snatched her hand away. She did not look at me or open her mouth, but that was the reminder I needed that she played for keeps.

In front of us were two ebony chests; the lids had been removed and lay next to the chests. One chest was for Pah and one was for me, no doubt, but for what purpose? I didn't have long to wait; musicians began to play a tune on their skin drums and string and wood instruments. How I loved the sound of the wood instruments, so lonely, so forlorn. It sounded like my heart! Tears brimmed in my eyes as I scanned the crowded tent. I loved these brown and olive-skinned faces. I loved the Meshwesh; we were family, tied together by the blood of Ma and the hope of a prosperous future at Zerzura.

Our father spoke now, "Come now, Meshwesh. Bless the anni-mekhmas as they prepare for their next trial. If you have a gift to offer, place your gift inside one of the chests and please bless the anni-mekhma who will receive your gift as you leave." He greeted the people as they approached us. He touched the heads of the children and kissed the cheeks of the older women. Father was always careful to show all due respect to the people, for it was them he served. After the offerings were collected, the chests were closed. Both of us had received quite a few gifts, enough to show that the people truly loved us, but I could tell Pah had received more than I. More evidence that I had no skill at politics. Apparently many still trusted her, despite this morning's controversy.

No matter. I can overcome this!

Farrah stood in the center of the tent and prayed to our ancestors for guidance. When the benediction ended, she invited Orba to address us. "Now, anni-mekhmas, the final test—the final trial has arrived! As mekhma, you must have the respect and trust of our neighbors and fellow tribes. We send you out now with our treasures to procure for us something of value. You can take no advisor, only yourself, your treasure and any supplies you may need. I now cast lots to determine who will go first and where." He shook his bag of ivory pieces and scattered them on the floor. He and Farrah peered at them, and Orba declared, "Nefret! You go to Biyat! Pah travels to Kemel. Go now! Represent your tribe!" The Meshwesh cheered, and the women clucked their tongues to show their approval.

Our father rose and stretched his arms out to us. Hugging us both, he surprised us with a rare show of emotion by kissing the tops of our heads. "Go now, my daughters. Have a care for yourselves and return to me."

"Yes, Father," we murmured and immediately left the tent. Camels had been prepared for us, and the treasures were poured into bags to hide their value from would-be thieves. I felt no fear; I felt nothing at all but grim determination. Feeling the pack and checking the saddle, I rearranged my bow so it would be nearer to me.

"Go now! Return to us, anni-mekhmas!" I petted my camel, who sat obediently waiting for me. Paimu ran to me crying; her small arms flew around my waist. At that moment, it occurred to me that I had not properly dressed for the day. My sister's hair was brushed and gleaming, yet mine was still in my sleeping braid. I sighed. Nothing to be done about that now.

"You promised me, princess! That I would never be without you. You cannot leave me. I will go with you! See—I have sandals and can run very fast. Please!"

Ayn stood behind her, looking exasperated. "I am sorry, anni-mekhma, but she would not listen to me."

I smiled at the child and waved a hand at Ayn to calm her. "Not this time, my monkey. I have to ride very fast to Biyat, too fast for a monkey like you."

"I can ride fast. I know I can! Please, don't leave me, Nefret." She sobbed now, and even Ayn's heart began to melt. She stroked the girl's hair and spoke softly to her.

"I cannot take you, Paimu, because if I do, the tribe at Biyat may want to keep you. I am there to make a trade, am I not? You are my treasure, Paimu. I could not bear to lose you. Now please listen to me. Stay with Ayn and help her. Teach Alexio how to climb the palm if you like."

That answer seemed to satisfy her. "When will you be back?"

Alexio passed by Pah and joined us, answering her, "Three days unless she stays the night." He cast his lovely eyes on me and said, "It's a straight shot, Nefret. Follow the sun and you can't miss it. I packed a knife in your hip bag, just in case. Do not stop for any reason until you get to Biyat. It is a long day's ride, but you can do it easily."

I climbed on the camel, hoping to avoid any further gossip about my relationship with Alexio. Still, I wanted to fling my arms around him one last time. I thanked him politely and walked the camel to the edge of the camp. Pah rode away, a boisterous crowd of young people cheering for her as she disappeared riding hard for the south. Now as I left the tribe behind, I heard cheers for me too; they were not as loud as Pah's, but they still warmed my heart and filled me with purpose. Waving goodbye, I scanned the faces for Father but did not see him. Kicking with my heels and clucking my tongue, I spurred the camel on and rode westward with all my might.

I rode steady for some time before the heat of the day began to burn my skin. Without dismounting, I covered my head with my worn brown cloak and took some refreshment from my goatskin. I drank the cool water and felt refreshed immediately, but my thirst quickly returned. In the distance my hot eyes spotted an unfamiliar small oasis. This would not be Biyat; it was too close to Timia. But if the occupants were friendly, perhaps I could take my rest there to avoid the midday sun.

I had traveled to Biyat when I was just a child, before I had breasts, and I remembered it well. Unlike Timia, which had a diamond shape, the Oasis of Biyat ran long and skinny, the lushness sprouting up around an underground stream. The sheltering land before me was nothing as large as Biyat and appeared as a clump of green grass in the midst of a sea of red sand. As I drew closer, I wrapped my cloth tighter around my face, hoping to avoid drawing unwanted attention with my red hair and green eyes.

"Kitch, kitch!" I clucked at the camel. I sat tall in the saddle despite my sore back and aching bottom. I drew close but not too close. Observing the oasis for a moment, my fears were allayed. The visitors were merely goatherds seeking to do the same thing as I was, find shelter from the heat. Riding closer, I called out in a friendly manner, "Peace to you."

"Peace to you as well!" A young boy called back and ran to find the goatherd, probably his father. Leading the camel to the water's edge, I settled under a palm and unwrapped my head. I splashed my face and hands, then set about searching for my lunch—chula bread and a cluster of dates from Timia. A crooked-backed old goatherd made his way to me, and his young protégé tagged along behind him. A third man hovered near the goats. My bow was on the other side of the camel, but my knife was on my side. I prayed I would not have to use it.

"Peace to you." The goatherd smiled politely and for a few minutes we exchanged pleasantries. But remembering Alexio's words, I did not tell more than I had to. The goatherd offered me some of his wine, but

I politely refused. Drinking wine in the heat of the day with strangers seemed a poor choice.

"What brings you to this little spot? There is nothing much here, sister."

Ignoring his attempt at friendliness I said with a smile, "I am only passing through."

"To Biyat, then?" He frowned, his forehead wrinkled with concern. The goatherd's face, like the faces of most who had spent their lives in the Sahara sun, was a map of lines and dark skin. "Oh no, do not go to Biyat. There are strange things happening. Go home. Go back to Timia."

"I did not say I was from Timia." I stopped unpacking my bag and stared at the old man.

"I can see plainly, red-haired one. These eyes have not failed me so far. Those are the colors of the Meshwesh," he said, pointing to my embroidered collar, "and they do love Timia this time of year. Tell me, does Farrah still live?"

"You know Farrah?"

He laughed as if he knew the most wonderful joke but had no intention of telling me. "Of course, of course, sister. And if you are here, that means she has yet to find Zerzura." He laughed even louder, as did his helper.

I had no desire to engage in more conversation with the goatherd, but I felt I had to know what dangers possibly lay ahead of me.

"What strange things do you mean?"

"Tall men, so tall they could touch the sky. A hot wind blows, hotter than any I have ever known. The Dancing Man has risen in the night sky, and a voice—a whispering voice—is carried on the breeze." He froze, his hand cupping his large ear as if he could hear it even now.

"These men, are they Nubians? The Nejd?"

He waved his hand as if I were stupid. "No Nubians— no Nejd." He muttered in a language I did not know and continued his story. "Tall they are, tall and spindly like these trees. And wherever they go, they sow unhappiness behind them. It is not wise to be out here by yourself, red-haired girl. These tall men come from beyond the southlands of Mut where no decent tribe dwells. They are at war with everyone! Go home now."

A chill crept down my spine, but I masked my fear. I nodded my thanks for his warning and offered him some dates; he happily accepted, thanking me profusely before he left.

Nervously, I watched the trio as surreptitiously as possible. If they were a danger to me, there was no need to boost their confidence by appearing afraid and vulnerable. As I sat under the tree and leaned against the trunk, I took out my blade and began to rub it with an oily cloth until it shone. I hoped they would spot the glinting metal and take the warning. It seemed they did, as they did not bother me again. The two older men rested under their makeshift tent while the boy cavorted with the goats until he too sought shelter. The bright day burned on. I ate my food and tried to stay awake, but the heat sapped the strength from my bones. I longed to brush out my hair and retie it, but doing so would not be wise. It would have to wait until I returned home or perhaps this evening if the people at Biyat were thoughtful enough to provide me with a bed.

My camel hunkered down, and I clucked at him playfully. Leaning back against the tree, I closed my eyes, thinking again of my dream. How real it had seemed to me! The coolness of the stone under my bare feet, the pounding of my heart as I turned each sharp curve in the confusing corridor. Would I ever forget seeing that fear reflected in the face of the boy who ran behind me?

Smenkhkare!

I felt my body relax and before I knew it, I had succumbed to sleep. I dreamed but did not remember it.

I awoke with a start, jolted awake by a noise that only my dream-self heard. Breathing hard from the rush of adrenaline, I found myself on my feet with my knife in my hand. I circled around the tree but saw nothing, no one. In fact, the others were gone, all three men and the dozen goats that accompanied them. I shielded my eyes with my hand and peeked at the sun. Hours had passed, but I did not know how many. It would be dark soon, and I did not want to be caught in the desert by the tall men the goatherd spoke of. And regardless, I had a job to do. I hoisted my supplies back in the saddle and climbed aboard the camel. Wrapping the cloth around my head, I continued my trek west, faster now as if giants indeed chased me.

I leaned into the camel, twisting the leather strap. I whispered in his ear, "Kitch, kitch!" Obediently, he ran faster, and I kept my spine straight and in line with his head. He ran as if he knew something I did not. As we hurried toward Biyat, I kept my eyes trained on the horizon, praying that I would see trouble before it approached me. How would I defend myself out here with no shelter and nobody I knew? I found myself missing Alexio again.

Focusing on the task at hand, I urged the animal forward and began to think about my trade. What would benefit my tribe? What was I expected to do? I had no idea, no inspiration, but I hoped that it would come to me when I needed it, just as it had earlier in the judgment of Ayn. My thoughts turned toward the Shining Man.

What if, like the fated "Queen of Zerzura," I was being tricked? What if my dreams were nothing more than dreams? It could not be true! His words were burned in my heart…

Will you trust me even when you cannot see me? When all others turn against you?

Time passed quickly as I rode. The sun hung low in the sky and soon it would be dark in the desert. If I did not arrive at Biyat soon I would be forced to sleep in the sand. As I cleared a tall dune, an acrid smell filled my nose. I gasped and stood amazed at the sight that lay before me. There were fires everywhere, and even from this distance I could see the charred remains of a camp.

My first instinct was to spur the camel toward the disaster, but the animal refused to obey me. Despite my attempts to convince him, he resolutely refused to take another step forward. Sliding off his back, I led him by the reins to get closer to the fiery scene. When I got as close as I dared, I stood still waiting and listening but could detect no sound except the crackling of fire. No one cried for help. I had to get closer. My unhappy camel tolerated my curiosity until we stepped into the camp. Then, with a snort, he pulled away from me and loped away. Clucking at him softly to calm him, I tied the strap to the tree and patted him, assuring him I would return. As he must have known, I needed him far more than he needed me. If he ran into the desert, he would easily find his way home. But without him, I would certainly perish.

I gagged as I walked into the camp. Quickly I balled my tunic's edge and covered my nose with it. The Meshwesh at Biyat did not belong to my tribe, but they were Meshwesh all the same. My stomach lurched as I walked past an avenue of scorched earth and debris that had once been tents. Walking carefully to avoid burning my sandaled feet, I paused every few feet to listen for calls for help or any sign that whoever did this was nearby.

Suddenly a thought occurred to me: what if the old man was right? What if this was proof that the "tall men" had been here? The Meshwesh obviously had not planned on leaving. The fire had consumed much, but many valuable things were left behind, like the clay pots that our women took pride in working. I picked up a broken one from the sand and rubbed the geometric patterns with my fingers.

I walked past one charred pile after another, my heart falling further in my chest with each step. "Hello?" I called. "Is anyone here?" My imagination could not muster a scenario of what must have taken place. Even if an uncontrollable fire had blazed through the camp, the Meshwesh would not have left their cooking pots or anything else. Yes, something evil happened here. The residue lingered.

"Hello?" I called again. Rising desperation forced me to dig deeper. I picked up a stick and used it to probe a smoking pile. I lifted the burned tent canvas and screamed. A tiny burned hand appeared, and I dropped the stick. Yes, this was the work of evil men. Feeling a surge of panic, I ran to the edge of the oasis hoping against hope that I would see a caravan in the distance, that I would see proof that someone had escaped. Leaving the green and brown grass behind me, I scurried up a small dune and climbed up to get a better look. Surely someone had escaped!

As I reached the sandy peak an intensely bitter aroma assaulted my senses. The smell of death rose up from the sand below me like a living thing. In a shallow valley were the bodies of my people. Dead Meshwesh covered the ground, their bodies half hidden in the sand. Mothers and fathers were tossed together with their children's limp bodies. Wicked gashes from unforgiving blades had opened their necks, and there were gaping spear wounds in their bellies. Falling to my knees, I cupped my mouth to prevent a scream from escaping. This was a place of death! Rocking back and forth, I could not turn my eyes from the carnage. Tears filled my eyes, and I let them flow unashamedly.

I don't know how long I stayed there on my knees in the deathly silence of the desert. My camel's long complaint called me back, and the reality that I was in danger came crashing down on me. There was nothing I could do for the Meshwesh before me, but what about my tribe? With one thought—save my people—I carefully slid down the sand to retrieve the evidence I needed. As I approached the first victim, a small boy whose face was hidden in the sand, I removed my knife from my belt. Quickly, I cut a piece of his singed garment away and tucked the cloth in my tunic. Sliding the knife back into place, my weariness vanished. It had been replaced by a surge of purpose and overwhelming fear.

My mission had changed. There would be no deal made here in this valley of death, but I cared not. The faces of the people I loved—Paimu, Alexio, Father and Pah—flashed before me. Could they now be in the path of whoever had mercilessly destroyed this tribe?

My legs ran hard and fast back to the camel. I threw myself in the saddle and, with a slap of my leather strap, spurred the animal toward home.

I prayed I was not too late.

Chapter Nine

The Girl Who Climbs—Paimu

"Paimu! Come down from there. It is well past time to eat!" Ayn called impatiently. I could tell by her expression that she was less than happy with me.

"Go away," I shouted from the top of the palm. I would never admit that I was afraid—too afraid to come down. Besides, the sun had set and Nefret had been gone for two days. I wanted to be the first to see her return with some great prize, for I had no doubt she would. Like Mahara who outsmarted the serpent and the winged lions to retrieve her clan's magic treasure, Nefret would not fail. She could not!

"You know she won't be back today. Be patient and come down. My mother has even made a honey cake just for you."

"No. Go away."

Ayn sighed in exasperation and then called up the tree again. "I suppose I could find Pah and have her come get you down, since I can't climb too well. She is probably rested from her travels."

A surge of panic hit my hungry belly. "I will come down now. The sun has gone away, and I cannot see anything anyway."

Ayn chuckled. "Indeed you cannot. Come now. Mother is waiting."

I crept slowly down the slick trunk, using my thighs and ankles to counterbalance my hands and arms. Somewhere below the tree were my shoes, a present from Nefret, my only true friend. With an impressive leap, I landed on the ground and wiped my dirty hands on my clothes.

Ayn crinkled her nose. "You smell terrible. When was the last time you bathed?"

With my hands on my hip I said, "You don't tell me when to take a bath! You are not my mother, Ayn!"

She grabbed my hand and pulled me with her. I struggled for a moment until her strong hand patted my behind. "Listen! Nefret asked me to take care of you, and that's what I am going to do. We can do this pleasantly, or you can make it hard on yourself. Which do you want?"

I snatched my hand away and rubbed it. It didn't really hurt, but I wanted her to know that I did not approve of her touching me. I did not care to be touched unless I did the touching. Even Nefret did not touch me. "I know you don't really want me with you, Ayn. Nobody ever does. Why shouldn't I smell like the goats? Even Nefret gave me away! I am just your punishment." I had not intended to vent such emotion, but the words tumbled out of my heart before I could think about them.

She tilted her head and gazed down at me. Ayn was not a pretty girl, not like Nefret with her dark red hair, olive skin and cat's eyes. Even Alexio was prettier than Ayn, but she was strong and brave—and foolish, as she proved the other day.

Ayn stood much taller than me. In fact, she stood much taller than all the girls her age, but she did not seem to mind or notice. In comparison, I felt small, very small indeed. "Maybe you are right, and maybe you are not," she observed. "I do not know. I do know I gave my word to the anni-mekhma, and I will not fail to keep it. I do not mean you any harm, Paimu. I would very much like to be your friend if you have room for one more." I pushed my bangs from my eyes and stared at her, hoping to perceive any ill will she might have held for me. She had never cared to speak to me before, and now she wanted to be my friend?

Ayn's eyes shifted, and I turned to see what she spotted. Was it Nefret? My heart leaped, but only for a moment. It was not Nefret but Pah who walked toward us, now washed and dressed like a mekhma in a blue gown that revealed one perfect shoulder. The gold thread embroidery at the sleeves and neck made me think of Mahara's magical gown.

"Is this one giving you trouble, Ayn?" Pah purred as she reached out and absently stroked my messy hair. "You *can* handle her, can't you?"

Ayn reached for me, snatching me away from Pah. I did not argue with her this time or lecture her on how I did not like being touched. Pah frightened me, and she always had. Maybe it was because I dreamed about her once—she'd run toward me, first with her own face and then with the face of a snarling bear.

"No trouble at all, anni-mekhma." Ayn took my hand protectively and murmured, "Excuse me." We had taken only a few steps toward Ayn's home when Pah called my keeper back.

"I do not excuse you! That is all you have to say to me? You were my biggest supporter, Ayn. Now you turn your back on me when we are so close to reaching our goal."

Ayn stopped and glanced at me. "Go home. I will be there soon."

"No," I said, partly because I wanted to stand with her against Pah and partly because I wanted to hear what Nefret's sister had to say.

"Go now!" the girl commanded, and I walked away but only as far as the nearest tent. I squatted beside it in the shadows, hoping to hear what words they exchanged.

"How dare you accuse me of turning my back on you? You were going to let me die!"

"Nonsense, Ayn. Nefret would never have killed you— she doesn't have the stomach for such things."

Ayn snorted. "Ah, but you do. Don't you?"

"Yes." I saw the smile creep across Pah's face, and I shivered in the shadows. "I do. There is nothing I am not willing to do to be mekhma!"

In a sad voice, Ayn answered her, "I believe you, Pah."

"Do I still have your support, or do you like your new job as babysitter to Nefret's pet monkey?"

"Don't call her that, and I am not a babysitter."

Pah laughed. "Ayn, the great warrior, watching over orphans!" I saw Ayn's hand curl into a fist, but Pah did not seem afraid, not as I would have been. Pah bravely stepped toward the tall girl, and her shiny jeweled necklace glinted in the fading light. "You are called to a higher purpose, Ayn. You could be someone great, a woman-warrior that future generations will sing about. I will win. It is my destiny. I have brought home a great prize, far greater than any Nefret could buy or find. I am now mekhma in all but formality. Pledge your support to me again, while I have no doubts about you." I leaned forward to hear what Ayn would say, but a swatting hand smacked my bottom.

"Hey! You girl! Get away from there. What are you doing? Hoping to steal something? Go now!"

I ran from the woman's cruel hands and toward Namari's tent. I had nowhere else to go, unless I wanted to sleep in Nefret's empty tent. I did not like being alone at night—I was afraid of the dark. Or more truthfully of what waited in it.

What an evil woman! She made me leave my spot just when Ayn would speak and tell her true heart! I wanted to know the truth so I could tell Nefret when she arrived, but now I could not. Namari was waiting for me and presented me with the promised honey cake. Ayn's mother had been kind to me, kinder than most.

She crinkled her nose. "You need a bath."

"I know." I grinned at her as I smacked on the honey cake. My stomach rumbled loudly.

"You will have to take one tonight, little one, or you shall sleep with the goats."

I scowled but did not argue with her. Just once I would like to do what I wanted to do. Why had Nefret left me behind? Treasures of the tribe indeed! That was something the Meshwesh liked to say, but it was rarely true. At least not for an unwanted Algat girl who had nowhere else to go. I savored each morsel of the honey cake and finally licked my fingers clean.

"I will bathe in the pool tomorrow," I told her.

"No, you will bathe here tonight. See? I found a new tunic for you. You can wear it while we clean your other one. It belonged to Ayn when she was a girl." She held the tunic up to my chest and frowned at the ridiculous length. "We can shorten it a bit, and it will be perfect."

I couldn't help but smile. To have two tunics! How rich I would be! I removed my clothing and allowed Namari to wash my body. She complained and compared the skin behind my ears to the desert we lived in. "Have you left any sand in the desert, Paimu?"

I suffered through the scrubbing and endured the cold water. She scrubbed my feet with a camel hair brush, and I tried not to kick her as I laughed.

"Be still, monkey girl!"

"It tickles! I can't help it!"

She wanted to remain serious and focused on her task, but I could see a glimmer of a smile on her face too. It was a rare flash of happiness, and for a moment I pretended that Namari was my true mother. I enjoyed the fiction until her husband walked in. I grabbed the new tunic and clutched it to my naked body.

He did not acknowledge me but spoke tersely to his wife. "The anni-mekhma is back. I must go to see Semkah now. I do not know when I shall return." His strained face reflected worry, as did Namari's. I did not understand the exchange.

"Very well. Peace, husband."

"Peace to you, wife."

Without drying my hair or body, I slid the tunic on and searched for my sandals.

"Where do you think you are going?"

"I must go see Nefret."

She lit the lamp that hung from the center pole and laughed joylessly. "No, you *must* stay here. See, here is Ayn. Tell her that she must stay here—she is like a wild cat. The king's tent is no place for her."

"She is right, Paimu. I am sure Nefret will come when she can."

My fists clenched as I thought about what I should do next. Scream, set the tent on fire, kick Ayn and run? Nothing was clear except that Nefret had returned. "She is my friend. I have to see her." Tears filled my eyes.

"Shh…Paimu. Nefret has other matters to tend to besides you. I am sure she will come see you when she can. Take your rest now. If she comes while you are sleeping, someone will wake you."

Sullenly, I climbed into the pallet where I had slept the night before. I did not feel sleepy at all, but I could see that arguing with Ayn would get me nowhere. I cuddled up to the soft blanket and twisted the corner worriedly. The harder I strained to hear Ayn and Namari, the sleepier I became. The warm honey cake and cool bath had done their work on my tired body. I would never admit this to Ayn and her mother, but the feeling of being clean and having a new tunic comforted me more than I could have imagined.

Later, I awoke to the sound of Nari and Namari talking in hushed, worried tones. If it had been merely Namari and Ayn in the tent, I would have thrown back the blanket and demanded to know what they were talking about. I did not dare to speak to Nari in such a way. Remaining very still, I did not bother to push back the dark hair that had fallen in my face. I kept my breathing even and did not move. I was good at spying, a practice that made me feel powerful and safe. People always underestimated me.

"All of them?" Namari whispered.

"That's what she says. Run through with spears and their throats cut with a blade."

Nari's wife gasped and turned to look at Ayn and me. "What should we do? Where should we go?"

"Where *can* we go? There is nowhere to go, wife." He hugged her close and whispered in her ear. She nodded and put her arms around his neck. "I think the best thing to do is wait to hear what the scouting party discovers."

"I am surprised you didn't offer to go with them."

"Semkah prefers to keep me close by." He glanced at Ayn and she nodded, understanding the hidden message. Since Ayn's accusation, Nari's reputation as a faithful warrior and friend to Semkah had been tarnished. Even a child could predict that would be the result of such behavior.

"So what does this mean? Will they continue or wait until the scouts return?"

"I feel sure that Farrah will not want to wait, especially in light of this latest development. In her mind, we will need a mekhma to face whatever army may be advancing toward us."

"Yes, I can see that. You don't agree?"

"I think we should wait, but I have no voice on the Council. No influence with the king anymore. Nefret was not able to fulfill her trial. It seems only fair that we should wait. However, I am sure Pah will make a good mekhma. She is a strong leader. Always has been."

"So the Council has decided?"

Nari leaned back on his bed and pulled his wife to him. "Nothing is decided yet, but I can see which way the wind is blowing. Come here. Enough talk for now." They fell silent, and soon they both began to snore. The small oil lamp on the table flickered weakly until it burned away its fuel. I slid back my covers quietly and paused. My young heart beat wildly in my chest. I had to see Nefret. I had to, and no one would stop me!

Slowly I sat up. Nobody stirred and the snoring continued. I put on my shoes and stood. Ayn shifted on her pillow but did not wake. I walked to the tent flap and, as quickly as a Bee-Eater, stepped outside and ran through the dark, down the sandy pathway to find Nefret.

Aitnu strolled past me but did not spot me. He wore his battle gear, a leather tunic, a shield and his sword. Wrapped in his thoughts, he neither acknowledged me nor spoke to me, even when I thought his dark eyes fell upon me. I ducked behind a pile of saddles and heard him speak to two young men. They walked to the edge of the camp, with me following them as secretively as possible. The men selected camels, arranged the saddles and left under the cover of darkness. They headed west, presumably to Biyat.

As Aitnu and the other warriors rode away, I stepped out of my hiding place.

I felt a great sadness wash over me. Things were changing, and I did not like change. It always brought bad things.

It worried me that some of our warriors were leaving. Who would protect Nefret now? I raised my chin defiantly as I watched the men disappear into the thick darkness. I would go find Nefret! Focusing on my task, I stepped back on the path. I *had* to find my friend. Who else would help her if not me?

"Why am I not surprised to find you lurking about? Always in the way, always forgotten, aren't you, Paimu?"

Before my eyes could take in the darkened figure, I felt a pain in my stomach like I had never known. My hands flew to the spot, and with some shock I realized they were now wet.

Wet with blood.

Chapter Ten

A Marriage—Nefret

I squatted in the sand behind the lively fire that burned in the center of the circle. Across the fire, dozens of pairs of young eyes watched my every move with enjoyment. The marriage ceremony had been performed, and now the tribe made merry in honor of my sister and her new husband, Yuni. It seemed sacrilegious to celebrate when Meshwesh lay dead in the sand just a few days' ride away.

However, I was not the mekhma; I did not decide such things.

With her marriage to Yuni, Pah had offered the ultimate sacrifice, her own body on behalf of her people. I had failed my mission. I took comfort in the fact that the outcome had been out of my control. The gods had chosen the mekhma. Nothing could change that. I knew these things, but it left a bitter taste in my mouth. Everything would be different now, and no word came forth about my future.

Sitting in the place of honor were Father, Pah and Yuni. They clapped their hands in polite expectation of my tale. I bowed my head, keeping my eyes on my father—not on my sister whose eyes messaged her hate, and not on her husband, who made no secret of the fact that he lusted after every woman who passed in front of him.

The children clamored for my attention, and I stood, raising my hand to my forehead to my father, the host of the wedding festivities—this would be his last official event and, although no one openly expressed it, it would probably also be mine. He sat bare-chested, wearing only his robes of kingship and a skirt of dark blue. Father's long dark hair had been oiled, and it hung in rows of curls for the special day. He was a handsome man, my father. Pah whispered something to him and he laughed politely. The two shared their joke with Yuni, who laughed too. I did not let it discourage me. I walked toward the fire, my hands behind my back. Such small movements could hold an audience spellbound— at least I had this moment. I had a gift for storytelling, as Farrah told me when she remembered to speak to me at all. Mostly, she just stared at me.

"Daughter, tell us a story," Father said, smiling at me.

Slowly I began to dance as the drummer tapped a happy tune for me. I noticed Alexio's eyes watching as I waved my fingers and pointed my toes. Truthfully my dancing left something to be desired, but I could pose. Suddenly, I gestured with my hand and the drummer, an old, toothless man, stopped. I stood frozen, sneakily digging into my pocket. I grabbed a handful of purple flowers, the kind that spark and flame when tossed into a fire. I spun and tossed the flowers into the fire and stood staring at it. What was this? In the flames I could see again the dead bodies of the people of Biyat, thrown into the sandy valley to be left as food for the animals of the desert. I shook my head and closed my eyes. When I opened them, all eyes were on me.

"Aha!" I said quietly as the story I needed came to me like a living thing that had always been there, hanging in the air, waiting for the telling, as if this were the perfect time and place.

"Hear now, honored guests and treasures, the story of Numa, the woman who had no heart and therefore could not love. Ziza! Come!" I whispered to the little girl, "You must help me. Follow me, okay?" She gave me an embarrassed but willing smile and nodded her consent.

Again my heart broke.

Where could Paimu be? She should be here telling this story with me.

I missed my treasure, my monkey! I had not seen her in two days, and poor Ayn and I had been wracked with worry over her. Ayn swore that she had made every effort to keep her close, but the child had a mind of her own. I knew this to be true, so I did not lay this at Ayn's feet. Neither Namari nor Ziza's mother had seen the girl, and neither had any of her playmates. It was as if she had disappeared into thin air. Perhaps the Algat had returned to claim her? I prayed she had not been lost in the desert but merely was hiding from me to show her disapproval over my leaving her behind. Paimu had a strong will and a stubborn streak as wide as the Sahara.

Ziza scrambled to her feet and made the sign of respect to the king and my sister, just as I had. I patted her head and she knelt quietly beside me, ready to act out the story that I would weave. Ziza was an excellent young actress; in the past she had played the part of a monkey, a parrot, a lost traveler, a warrior princess and even the sun. She could do it all, but she was not my Paimu.

"Buried somewhere in the Red Lands is the body of Numa." I felt a cold chill and suddenly I saw a woman lying in the desert, the sand covering her face.

Who was she? I had never seen her before!

I shook my head and continued on, trying to regain my composure. "She was a beautiful woman, only she was born without a heart. She could not love. She could love neither husband nor children, nor her father or mother although they were honorable people. Numa would go out every day to pray for a heart. As often as she could, she would make a heart of bread and offer it to her tribe's deity, Washtu. She would lay it at the god's feet and return the next day, hoping to discover that the bread had turned into a real heart. Day after day, she rolled the bread, patted the bread and baked it into the shape of a heart. Each day was the same. No heart appeared. This was unfortunate because Numa was to be married in just three days. Her betrothed had great lands and much wealth. Numa desired to be a good wife and mother to the kind king's children.

"Numa had almost given up on receiving a heart. She wanted to love, to be in love, to feel love. She wanted to love others. It was her sole desire." I waved my hands and used my eyes to demonstrate how Numa must have felt. Beside me, Ziza pretended to bake a heart from sand and presented it to the fire.

"See? Day after day it was the same until one day, a jinn from a faraway land heard Numa crying. He dove down from his home in the clouds to see who this was crying in his domain. So surprised to see a woman without a heart, the jinn abandoned the sky and spoke to her.

"'Why do you cry, woman with no heart? If you have no heart, how are you able to cry?'

"'I can cry because tears don't come from the heart but from the soul. Love comes from the heart. I need a heart. Leave me be, jinn!'

"The jinn scowled at her and floated away. This happened for many days. The jinn flew by and came to speak to Numa. Finally, after a week of this, he asked her if she would accept a heart that he had made for her. Numa was suspicious, 'How can I trust a jinn? All jinn are notoriously evil' But even as she said the words, she was uncertain. Her father had always told her never to entertain a jinn, but this one offered her a heart. What should she do? Should she take the heart?

"The jinn flew away in a cloud of blue smoke, and Numa was relieved. But the jinn did not stay away for long. Two days later, on the eve of her wedding, he returned and presented her the heart again. Courageously, she refused to accept it. In this she was wise because it had been the jinn's plan to cause Numa to fall in love with him—the heart had been cast with an enchantment. Aggravated by her lack of trust, the jinn threw the heart at her feet.

"'See, I made this heart for you. If you do not take it, you will never have another one. Take the heart, woman, and experience love—but listen to me! You must swallow the heart before it will work for you. Also, know this, the first living creature you see after you have your heart is who you will love for eternity. Do not open your eyes until you are prepared to be in love. You have until sunset to decide. At that time, the magic of the heart will fail.'

"The woman watched the jinn sail up and up until he finally disappeared into the star-jeweled sky. It seemed like he had flown all the way to the moon. She looked at the heart on the ground, unsure what to do. Carefully she picked it up and dusted it off." Ziza dusted off an imaginary heart and pretended to examine it. "Numa kept her heart in a box, safe from anyone who might steal it. She told no one about the jinn or what she had been given. What should she do? Swallow the heart? Burn it? What if this was a trick to kill her?

"The hours were passing by, and Numa decided it would be better to take a chance on love than to live without it. More than anything, she wanted to love her husband! Numa did not know that the jinn secretly wanted her as his wife, even though marriage was forbidden between humans and jinn-kind. From a distance, the jinn watched her. She began to eat the heart he had made for her. She swallowed it as she stood outside the tent of her betrothed—the king she wished to marry. She called the name of the king, her future husband, and ran out of the tent to find him.

"When the jealous jinn saw this, he began to blow a wind with his angry lips. He blew so hard on the camp below that he created a storm above the oasis." I made the sound of wind, and Ziza bent and blew about like a palm. The children covered their eyes as the suspense grew.

"Despite her surprise and fear, Numa kept her eyes closed and felt the wind whip around her. She was afraid but did not dare open her eyes to see the destruction, afraid of what or whom she would fall in love with. The jinn traveled back down from the sky but unfortunately, the winds that he had created made this more difficult. He struggled to push through the wind and clouds to reach the human woman he desired but not before a lost donkey, frightened by the storm, ran past Numa and stepped on her bare toes. She screamed in agony and unthinkingly opened her eyes to see the backside of the donkey running away from her.

"All of a sudden, the heart began to speak to her, 'I love this donkey. I love this donkey's behind. I must love the donkey!'" The children began to laugh and howl at the joke. Ziza ran around the fire chasing an imaginary donkey, blowing kisses at it. The children rocked with laughter. I clapped my hands at her performance.

"The jinn, seeing that his trick had not worked, decided to move on to another camp to watch for another pretty woman who needed a heart. Here is the lesson, dear ones. If you happen to meet a jinn who offers you a heart, refuse it. It is merely a trick, and you may end up loving a donkey!"

The kids clapped at the story, and even my father had a good chuckle. The listeners showed their appreciation by tossing coral-colored desert flowers at my feet. I took Ziza's hand and we hugged, plainly pleased with ourselves. We collected our flowers and returned to sit near the bridal couple in a reserved place of honor. Pah made a space for me beside her at the feast, but I could see she had not enjoyed my story. She gripped my wrist and whispered fiercely, "You call Yuni a donkey, sister? Why would you tell such a story at my wedding feast?"

"Such was not my intention, dearest. But he looks much like a donkey, doesn't he?" Suddenly Pah rose and stared down at me fiercely. I thought she would slap me, as she had before, but she raised her hands and invited all the young women present to join her in a dance. I did not join her, and she did not invite me. I was not trying to find a husband, as many of the girls here were. My father looked at me questioningly, but I shook my head. His words from an earlier conversation echoed in my mind: "Please, Nefret. Marry so your sister cannot send you away. If you were betrothed to someone, she would have no power over you." I had given him a weak smile but refused.

Alexio plunked down in Pah's empty spot. "Nefret, you should watch yourself. Don't provoke her," he whispered, pretending to offer me a cup of wine.

"I am not provoking her. I told a story." I handed the cup back to him and clapped for the dancers. Alexio and I had grown apart in recent months, but in the past few days, things had changed. Looks passed between us that I could not readily explain. At times, he looked at me like a hungry man who had returned to the oasis after spending a month lost in the desert. Sometimes I thought he would ask me something, but I did not make that easy.

Somewhere in this crowd was Farafra, his intended. She made no friendly overtures to me, nor I to her. She stared at Alexio constantly but danced with the others, hoping he would notice her. Alexio was tall, with strong arms and legs, a requirement for a young man who wished to be a trader. He could carry sacks of heavy wheat and boxes of goods with little effort. He had smooth, light brown skin and dark eyes with a thick fringe of lashes. He had an easy, friendly manner and a pleasant, deep voice. The dance continued, and we smiled and clapped along.

My beautiful sister appeared to be the happiest woman alive; only I knew her unhappiness. I loved Pah and hoped she would soon forgive me. I had not intended to hurt her. Perhaps it had been a foolish story choice for a wedding, but as far as I could see, she was the only person who had been offended by the telling.

When the dance ended, one of the Council would come and declare good things over the marriage of Pah and Yuni and all would forget about me. It was good to be forgotten.

As if a veil had been lifted from my eyes, I became aware that someone watched me. I searched for Alexio, who had walked away to talk to nearby friends, but it was not him. Now that the dance had ended, he talked and laughed with Farafra. She was pretty, graceful and charmingly breathless after her dance; I felt a momentary stab of jealousy but pushed it away. Why shouldn't Alexio be happy? The girl was his intended, and she certainly appeared smitten with him. He caught me staring and smiled. Embarrassed, I looked away and continued to scan the crowd. The feeling that I was being watched did not fade.

I began to feel more uncomfortable even as I hunkered down into a cushion, tossed my long copper curls behind my back and slapped a smile on my face. Sitting cross-legged, I looked into the darkness beyond the crowd and thought I saw a figure move at the edge of the camp behind my father's massive tent. The height and size of the figure surprised me. And whoever he was, he had unusual eyes; it was like looking into the shiny eyes of a panther. Instinctively, I crossed my fingers to guard against evil magic. Before I could speak or call someone, the eyes faded and the figure disappeared. My heart pounded in my chest like a trapped bird. Everything around me—the smell of burning wood from the fire, the noise of the instruments, the chattering of the people—faded into nothingness. I shot to my feet on wobbly knees. I took a few steps toward the spot where the shiny-eyed being had stood, but I did not step into the darkness. I glanced behind me at my tribe, who continued in their revelry apparently unaware of the visitor. My mouth opened; I thought I should yell to someone, to warn them, but what would I say?

Then another face caught my attention. It was Farrah—perhaps she had seen him too. But she made no gesture and only watched me curiously. Maybe she had not seen anything after all.

I felt the urge to disappear, so I scurried away to my tent. It was time for this night to end. But that was not to be; Pah followed me. I stood on the path and laughed at her. "You are leaving your own wedding party? What will your husband say, Pah?"

"At least I will have a wedding—what will you have, Nefret? You won't have Alexio!" A beautiful smile spread across her face. It doubly stung that a face so like my own should mock me.

"None of us knows what the future holds, Pah. Are you the Old One now? Can you see the future?"

She laughed aloud. "You believe that? She can't see anything. Nothing at all. I don't need the Old One's sight to know you won't have Alexio as a husband. I am the mekhma now! You will marry whom I tell you to marry."

"I shall not marry anyone! What do you want, Pah? You have it all now."

"I want an apology! You had no right to tell such a story at my wedding. Apologize now!"

It was my turn to laugh. "What?"

"You *will* apologize, Nefret. Apologize to your mekhma while you still can." Her voice dropped to a deadly whisper. She inched closer, and the scent of expensive oils wafted around her.

I stared into the face of my first friend and now my greatest enemy. It was as if time stopped for a moment. She stood poised and ready to hear my apology, a proud, victorious look on her face.

"I would rather die." I tilted my chin and matched her stubborn expression.

Her lips set in straight lines, and anger flashed in her dark green eyes. "That can be arranged." She turned on her heel and slung her cloak over her shoulder before marching back to her wedding feast. My hands and body shook as I watched her walk away. There were no tears in my eyes, only emptiness in my heart. I would have to leave. I feared what Pah might do to the people I loved. I quickly returned to my small tent. I needed to pack for my journey.

Paimu! For a second, I imagined the worst. Did Pah have something to do with the girl's disappearance? Could she be that cruel?

I saw a figure waiting for me outside my tent. I froze, thinking it might be the frightening visitor I spotted earlier. But as I drew closer I recognized the tall figure as my father's. "Nefret!" he whispered.

"Come in, Father." We walked inside together, and I decided then and there to tell him nothing. He could not suspect my intentions, for I knew he would try to stop me. If the Meshwesh were to follow the Old Ways, then I would be turned away properly and with the tribe's blessing. That I could not bear. I would rather leave in the night without any type of sendoff. If only I could find Paimu! How could I leave without saying goodbye to her?

"Nefret, I urge you to reconsider your decision. If you marry someone honorable from Omel's tribe, Omel will surely welcome you and you will live with them for the rest of your life or until we return to Zerzura. Please consider this. Much is changing, and I can no longer protect you from your sister."

"I know that you care for me, Father, but I have no desire to marry anyone."

"If you spoke kindly to your sister, I am sure she would make the arrangements if you have your heart set on some young man." I did not answer him. "Please…" For the first time in my life, I saw my father cry. I touched his hand, and he pulled me to his chest and held me close. His hand clutched the back of my head gently as he wept. "I can't bear to lose you. You are so like your mother, did you know? You have her kind heart, and she loved children as you do. What would Kadeema say if I let you wander away into the Red Sands? She saw all this and could not bear it. Now I must bear it alone."

Shocked at his emotional outburst, I did not know what to say; I let his tears soak over me until soon I shed my own. "Father, I think it is too late. Pah is determined to see me gone, and I will not disappoint her."

Breaking our embrace, Father wiped the tears from his eyes with the back of his hand. He paced the small tent. "My brother, damn him! Insisting on the Old Ways! I would challenge him if I thought it would change anything."

"What is done is done. I am not afraid," I lied with false confidence.

His hands on his hips, he paused his pacing and looked at me. "You should be. These are strange times. You have seen it with your own eyes, and it is even more dangerous for a woman traveling the desert by herself."

"What do you mean?"

"In the best of times, the desert is no place for a single traveler, but that is especially true now with these attacks."

"Can't you call all the tribes here? What if we all stood together against these tall men or whoever is behind this?"

"This oasis is not large enough to support all the Meshwesh. I wish there was another way." He squeezed my shoulders and stared me in the eye. "When you leave, go to Petra. It is five days from here, far to the north. Go there and present yourself to the Nabataean king. Take this sigil with you and tell him who you are—he will honor me." I accepted the small painted banner.

"You want me to go to Petra? Isn't that the home of the jinn?"

"Superstition. Myth. There are no jinn, Nefret. If there ever were, they are long dead now. You should fear the living rather than spirits."

"Very well, Father. I will go to Petra."

"When I can, I will send someone to you with supplies. Pack what you can carry, but don't overburden yourself. Remember what you know. You have been taught well.

You can make it, Nefret and I promise that I will not leave you alone."

I hugged him. He said, "In the meantime, do not push your sister. Pah holds all the power now, and she has very little love for you, although I cannot understand why."

With a final squeeze of my shoulder, he left me alone. Despite the distant music and the laughter that echoed through the camp, I decided to lie down for a nap. My plan was to rest now and rise early, earlier than even the goatherds. I would leave in the morning and head north to Petra, just as father instructed me. Although fear gripped my heart, I felt some comfort knowing the depth of his love.

I lay down on my pallet and gazed up at the dried flowers that hung from the center pole, Alexio's gift to me. I would miss him. I would miss dear Paimu. I hoped that when she came out of hiding, she would forgive me for leaving. The more I thought about it, the more I suspected that Ziza had hidden her at Paimu's request. As my eyelids drooped, I thought about what I would leave her.

She needed new shoes, but I had none that would fit her. Instead, I would leave her my silver bracelets and a few of my gold coins. To my father, I would send my necklace, the treasure that I had found in the desert.

To Alexio, well, I wasn't sure what to leave him.

I had already given him my heart.

Chapter Eleven

Death—Farrah

My bones hurt, my body and mind felt ... I could not refuse the dead girl who stood by my bed.

Her face was gray, her lips were bloodless and her eyes were like bottomless pits of darkness. The girl demanded revenge.

When I first awoke, I thought my spirit-visitor might be Ze, but the dead girl was too small and too young to be my sister. Ze had died as a young woman, not as a child. I lit a candle, and the ghost stepped back, fleeing from the light. She was not ready to leave the shadows until this matter had been settled.

"Paimu!" Realization crept across my face. Without acknowledging what I had said, the dead girl stepped to my tent door and vanished. I followed after her into the darkness. Mina slept at the foot of my bed, but I did not rouse her.

I strained to see into the gloom; an unusual fog had rolled into the camp, making it difficult to see even my own feet. "Where are you, girl?" I whispered into the darkness. Even before the words settled into the air around me, the dead girl reappeared, the fog clearing a bit to reveal her shocking face. "Where are we going? Are you taking me to my death, child?" My heart trembled at the thought.

She raised her finger to her lips. I kept quiet as she led me—a growing feeling of dread cascaded over me. Still I journeyed on behind her. I followed her down the sandy path to the center of the camp. We stood before Pah's tent door. The girl stepped through the canvas, and I followed her by slipping through the tent opening. How ironic that the mekhma's guards were asleep at their post! Surely that was this spirit's doing. Inside were Pah and her stupid husband Yuni, the pair sleeping soundly on a pile of luxurious furs.

I stood over the mekhma and watched as the girl pointed. Ah! Pah had murdered the child, and now Paimu had come for her revenge.

I nudged the sleeping queen with my toe and she awoke with a start, her dark copper hair tangled around her face. "What is it? What are you doing here? Who let you in?"

"They sleep, mekhma…and you have blood on your hands."

Still sleepy, Pah rubbed her face. "What? What are you talking about, Old One? Can't this wait?"

Anger welled up inside me. Was it mine? Was it Paimu's? I did not know. "Standing next to you is the child. The child you murdered and left in the sand. How did you kill her, mekhma? With a dagger? Ah yes, I see her wound." My hand flew to my stomach, matching the child's movements.

Pah flew to her feet and said in a whisper, "Lies! You must have a fever, Old One. Now go back to your tent. Do as I command!" She feigned outrage, but I could see the truth in her eyes. She had done this thing! I laughed at her.

The thin red-haired girl ordered me back to my tent again, and still I laughed but not at her. I laughed because it was I who had created all this misery. I had selected Pah over Nefret. I had chosen poorly.

"Stop that! Leave now, Farrah! Before I have you removed! Guards!"

Had I not held her first when she entered this world, even before her parents? *I* had spoken the words of life over her—*I* had predicted her rise as mekhma, and this was how she spoke to me.

"You do *not* command me, young one! As easily as I raised you, I can bring you down. And…" I said with a dark laugh, "you cannot deny justice to the dead. Believe me, I know. Murder exacts a price, even from mekhmas."

"What is going on here?" Yuni, Pah's big-eared husband, reached for his tunic and rose from his bed.

"Out!" I shouted at him.

"What?" he said, his hands on his hips, unashamed of his nakedness.

"Order him to leave, Pah, or he may hear something he cannot un-hear."

Furrowing her brow, Pah told her husband, "Go now, Yuni. All is well, my love." Her eyes never left mine.

He dressed quickly and left us, pausing once at the door. "Should I call someone?"

Pah smiled at him peacefully. "No, call no one. I will come find you." I gave her credit; she had all the skills of a great actress. She reached for her robe, sliding it over her body; her hands had disappeared into the voluminous fabric. With a dainty smile so like her sister's she said, "Now explain yourself, Farrah."

"I wonder how Yuni would feel if it were known that his new wife had come to her marriage bed opened by another man. I care little for these things, but for a mekhma who has pledged to follow the Old Ways, and who came to power under them…"

"You would not dare!" Pah stood so close to my face I could feel her breath on me. The heat of her anger astonished me, but I refused to shudder before one so young.

"Wouldn't I?"

"If you knew, why wait until now to speak of it?"

"As I said, the condition of your maidenhood is of little concern to me. Although it might be interesting to see your father's expression when he hears who plucked the fruit from the vine. However, I care little about this matter, and that is not why I came here."

She eased back a step and drew up her gown with her hands as she stepped back again with narrowed eyes. "Why then have you come, Old One?"

"I awoke with a dead girl standing over me—Paimu, Nefret's treasure. She led me to you."

Her eyes widened again and her lips set in a grim line. She said nothing, so I continued.

"You murdered her, Pah—although your motives for doing so are unclear to me. And fortunately for you, the dead do not speak. Whatever your intentions, you must confess your crime and tell us where you hid her body or else you walk under a curse. You had no authority to do such a thing."

"Lies!" Pah hissed, but I heard the truth in her voice. And the dead girl's pale face testified against her.

Although the mekhma could not see her, I could. Awareness crept over me—I could see again!

"This was a shameful act, a poor way to begin your rule, Pah hap Semkah. Perhaps your tribe will forgive you, but you cannot hide from this deed. The dead have come seeking vengeance."

"She wasn't even Meshwesh!"

"Paimu was a treasure of the tribe," I said firmly. Terror flashed in her eyes, but she quickly recovered.

"Now, Farrah. I understand that you think you see things—that you're some type of nabi-prophetess. But the truth is you are getting old. Too old, I am afraid, to lead the Council anymore. How can we trust your judgment when you tell such lies? Now go rest, and I will send someone to attend you. You are weak from the trials, Old One."

The dead child stepped closer to us, staring at Pah's face and then at mine. She shook her head at me furiously, but I could not determine what she wished to convey. Hot anger rose in my gut, and I would not be denied this confrontation. The reality of what I had done, how I had swayed the Council to favor Pah, all my deeds weighed on me now as the truth of her character was revealed to me. I had to make this right!

"How dare you speak to me in such a manner? I am not your foolish husband, nor am I one of your stupid followers, Pah. What could that child have done to you? What crime could she have committed that would have caused you to take her young life—to shed her blood in the sand? I see her! I see the wound in her belly! Confess the truth now!"

"Now you turn your back on me? I only did what you taught me!" Her voice sounded sharp as steel.

"I never taught you to murder, Pah."

"Oh? Didn't you? What do you think the flames showed me, Farrah? I could see very well. I know your secret." Her voice dripped venom. "The flames showed me the day you sat on my grandfather Onesu's chest, spat in his face and slid the knife across his neck! How dare you lecture me! Have you not done the same thing?"

My voice shook with anger. "No! It is not the same thing! I never killed a child! I took vengeance for my sister, something you would know nothing about! How easy was it, Pah, to turn your back on *your* sister? To kill her treasure?"

"Again with Nefret? You were the one who wanted me to win the trials, and so I have! I am the strongest, the fastest, the smartest—but does that matter to you? Nobody ever saw me. Not Alexio, not Semkah, no one! I made a name for myself, and I will never relinquish my power! You have no right to ask me! You are not innocent, Farrah."

Blinking away her accusations, I asked her again, "What did you do, Pah? I must know what happened. You cannot take us to Zerzura with this stain on your soul. The way will be hidden from you unless you confess. You must trust me in this."

"Why should I tell you anything? You don't know what you're talking about, Farrah! Now leave, or I *will* call my guards to haul you out of here." Turning her back on me, she strode to a nearby table and began brushing the tangles from her hair. From the reflection in the brass mirror she held, I could see her pretty face. It appeared calm and fearless, but I knew better. I stepped behind her.

"Do not turn your back on me, girl!"

"I am going to warn you only once more." She stared at me from the mirror. "Leave now, Farrah."

"You cannot send *her* away. You took a life—a debt is owed."

Setting down the brush, she turned to face me. We were inches apart. Out of the corner of my eye I could see Paimu slipping away, her image fading, her mouth open in a silent scream. As she backed away, sadness washed over her face. I reached out my hand to the dead girl to plead with her to remain, but I was unable to express my words.

A shocking pain caused my body to seize all thoughts and feelings. I was consumed by the pain, and my hands clutched at the source of the agony. A blade protruded from my belly. Pah's hand was upon it.

With an anguished gasp, I stared into the mekhma's lovely face. Her lowered lids shielded her eyes, eyes that watched me fall to my knees. A smile crept across her full, apricot-colored lips. As I fell, she twisted the blade once more before she slid it from my body. I wanted to scream but found no voice. This was my end. I kept staring at her face, and she never swayed from my vision.

Mina, if you can hear me. Come now!

I could not speak the words, but my mind called Mina to me. Sometimes she could hear me; perhaps it was not too late.

Mina, please. Come!

Pah knelt beside me. "Now I take *my* vengeance, Farrah. I can see in the flames, remember?" She whispered into my ear, "I saw what you did to my mother. How you led her to the dream world even though you knew it would kill her. You left her there. Then you watched as she walked into the desert and was swallowed by the sand. You have more than one death on your hands, don't you, Old One?"

I tried to explain myself, but the only sound I made was a weak gurgle. I could barely breathe now. Death would arrive any second—excruciating pain radiated from my belly to all parts of my body. I could feel my heart pounding harder and the blood flowed faster.

"You deserve death. How dare you think you could take this from me? I am the mekhma! I *am* the life of the Meshwesh! It is not in your power to stop what the gods have ordained—you who worship dead ancestors. What have they ever done for you, Farrah? I worship the true gods of Kemet—Isis, Hathor and Mut! It is them you have offended with your unholy prayers and deeds. Go now, Old One, and may you never find your ancestors. Reap now what you have sown!"

Mina!

The taste of blood filled my mouth, and the light began to fade from my vision. All that was left for me was the face of Nefret…no, that was Pah's face above me, gloating and victorious.

I curse you, Pah.

From behind her, a sound—a muffled scream. Mina stepped into view and pushed the mekhma aside. She did not speak. I sometimes wondered if she had forgotten how. I missed hearing her voice, so deep and dusky, quite different than what one would expect from such a plain face. I reached for her, but my hands would not obey. She pulled me to her and shook with silent cries as the light dimmed to just a pinhole. My garment felt sticky and wet.

There would be no justice for Paimu now. That thought saddened me.

Even worse than the pain was the knowledge that I would never see Zerzura again. Not in this life or the next.

My misery was complete.

Chapter Twelve

Outcast—Semkah

I was riding the blue waves of the Northern Sea again—I knew this dream. Each time it unfolded differently, but always I would see Kadeema in the distance and rarely did I reach her. This time, the motion of the waves did not leave me retching on the deck like a pregnant woman. No salty waves threatened to drown me as they had when I was a young man and in other dreams. In this dream, things were different. That both worried and excited me.

I stood at the bow of the boat confidently, watching the land of Grecia become larger and larger as I drew near its shores. I had a crew, but their faces were elusive, likely unimportant to the drama that was about to unfold.

I scanned the hills knowing that I would see her. Yes! There she was—high on a hilltop, the highest hilltop. *Kadeema!* Behind her, her long red curls bounced on the breeze and her bare arms were open and welcoming to me. Too far away to see the expression on her face, I imagined it, peaceful and serene. Her coral lips parted as she whispered my name.

"Semkah! Semkah! Hurry, my love!" Her straight, proud nose and wide green eyes set her apart from any of the women I knew.

Suddenly, a mist threatened to cloud my view—I frantically waved my hands and unexpectedly the fog disappeared. I laughed with joy when I discovered that the boat now rested very close to the shore. Soon I would disembark and run up the hill to find her—to be with her again at long last.

"Not long now, Kadeema!" I called up to her.

I waved furiously at her as the boat's anchor fell into the water with a loud splash. The cruel sun rose behind her, and again I could not see her face. Frustration rose within me. To look upon her face again! Her arms were not outstretched anymore; they were at her side, and her hair no longer floated around her. Something was wrong! She was leaving—somehow I knew it!

Desperately I leaped from the boat into the water. With all my might I swam for the shore, knowing that the time grew short. Splashing to the shore desperate for breath, I forced myself to stand. I shed my dagger and heavy wet tunic and climbed the hillside on wobbly legs like a drunken man. "Kadeema!" I called, but no answer came. Higher and higher I climbed, navigating sharp rocks and slick muddy patches. Finally reaching the grassy precipice, I stopped to catch my breath before making the last push to the top of the hill. Too winded to speak, I licked my dry, salty lips and threw myself on the crag.

No one was there. I wept as a man should not, without shame or care for who might witness my weakness. When I had no more tears to shed, I rolled over on my back and stared at the gray sky above me. "Kadeema!" I yelled furiously. "Why have you left me again?"

The clouds lowered, as they could do only in dreams, until they rested right above me. They moved and shook and parted, and I saw her face again. This time I saw it as clearly as I could see anyone's, only it hovered above me from the clouds.

"Why are you here, husband?"

Surprised and troubled by her question, I smiled at her. "My wife! How I have longed to see you, to touch you!" With shaking fingers I reached for her, but she pulled away. "Come to me, Kadeema. I thought I would never find you."

Her face grew sad. "You should not be here, Semkah. This is no place for flesh and blood, my love." Her face began to disappear from my sight.

"No! Why do you flee from me?"

She stared back, her face a mask of solemnity. There was no life there, no desire for me, just sadness and regret. How many times had I traveled here in my dreams and prayed for such a moment? Without moving her lips she whispered, "They're coming…protect my daughters, Semkah. If you love me, protect them." She bowed her head, and disappeared, swallowed into the mist that threatened to take me as well. The fallen cloud was freezing to the touch, and my skin crawled as it threatened to envelop me. I began to run—I did not know where—anywhere but into the mist. As I moved, it rolled behind me like a living thing. I could hear the screams and moans of others trapped in the rolling wall of gray that covered the hill. I ran to the cliff's edge—I had nowhere else to go. As the gray cloud darkened to black and reached for me, I leaped. I screamed and woke up to find Omel standing over me.

"Brother! Wake up! Your daughter calls you!"

"Nefret? I thought you were going home."

"No, not Nefret. It is Pah who has summoned you. I wished to do just that thing, but my son Alexio has ridden out—foolish boy. He has no patience and did not tell me that he was leaving. I cannot leave without him."

"Ridden out where?"

"He is impatient to prove Nefret's story. He rode to Siya for other proof instead of waiting for Aitnu's return from Biyat. Foolish boy! But it is good that I have not left, because Farrah, the Old One, has disappeared along with the other—the Algat girl. That is two disappearances in two days! Something is wrong here at Timia." Omel paused, and his long legs shuffled nervously as if he did not want to tell me something. Ignoring his Egyptian skirt and kohl-lined eyes, I observed him carefully.

"Well, what is it?"

"Nefret left in the night. From the tracks in the sand, it appears as if she traveled to the north. She can easily be found, my brother. Should I go and bring her back? I am sure the mekhma would want to send her off properly, according to the Old Ways."

"Indeed I am sure she would not." I said wearily, Kadeema's condemning eyes still before me. Now was the time for truth, wasn't it? I would never see Kadeema again, and my daughters were now mortal enemies. I had allowed this to happen. "Don't go after her. I will deal with the mekhma. Now that she has been elected by the Council, the mekhma isn't going to follow the Old Ways, I can assure you of that. No way will she want the tribe to shower Nefret with their silver and gold and send her away happily. Nefret did the right thing, Omel."

"I don't think your other daughter agrees…" he said, continuing in a hushed voice, "and you should not say such things to others, even to me. That could be considered treason now that we have a mekhma."

"Then let her send me away too. I am too tired, too old to worry about hurting my daughter's feelings—and I would feel the same way even if she were the Queen of Egypt!" A chill ran up my spine, and I got up and sloshed cold water on my face in an attempt to purge my mind and heart of the dream. "What has happened to Farrah? Another trip into the desert? Some kind of ritual that she has told us nothing about? She has done this before, disappearing for days and then showing up unharmed. What does her acolyte say?"

"Nothing, of course. We cannot question her—she took the oath."

"Yes, I know."

Omel said, "This is not like before. Farrah did not simply walk off the oasis."

"What makes you say that?" I rubbed my face with the linen towel and reached for my belt.

"Because there is blood in the sand, much blood. One of the dogs found the trail but so far not Farrah."

The tribe would be rattled by this news. Too much was happening—it could only mean that our fortunes had turned and not for the better.

"You should hurry, brother, and be warned. I am afraid we have awakened a fierce hawk in Pah."

"Not *we*, brother. This was not my idea. It was you who wanted Pah. It was you who wanted to use the Old Ways when it was advantageous to you. Now I must go and deal with her."

As I slid my dual blades into my leather harness, I glanced at my snake tattoos. Although the purple ink had faded, it was if they were alive today, alive and ready to protect me from my own ambitious child. I hoped they would.

With sadness from the dream lingering in my mind and heart, I walked to Pah's tent and waited to be welcomed in. Pah had chosen blue as her fabric for her royal tent, with a gold top and rich gold cords that streamed from the center pole. Ushered in speedily, I took in my surroundings quickly. My daughter had not wasted any time setting up her tent. A small backless chair sat near the center of the tent, like a throne. So this was how it was to be, then? Not mekhma but queen?

She came into the tent behind me and took her seat in the chair. Spreading her blue gown about her, she sat serenely enough, but I could tell a storm brewed within her. "Father, is it true that you sent Nefret away? Before our tribe could bless her properly?"

"I advised Nefret to marry; that is all. She refused and declared her intentions to leave. I counseled against it, but she was resolute. There was no persuading her."

Pah was not fooling me; I knew perfectly well that she had no intention of blessing her sister before she left. "More is the pity," she said, "because now she stands accused of murdering our beloved Farrah and probably Paimu too."

A laugh flew out of my throat. "I can't believe that! Nefret would never harm any creature—especially Paimu! She loved the girl like a…I mean…like a…"

"Like a sister?"

I turned red. I did not want to stir Pah to jealousy over poor Paimu.

"Now, just now, we have found the body of Paimu, and we have found the body of Farrah. Both were stabbed with a knife, stabbed in their bellies. Nefret is missing. No one has seen her. Isn't that suspicious?"

"It is unfortunate, but I do not think it suspicious. Are you bringing some sort of charges against your own sister, daughter?"

Pah's wide, innocent-looking eyes had deceived me before; I would not fall for it again. She would do what she wanted, but now I had to think of Nefret.

Without answering me, she pressed on. "And Alexio? Am I to believe it is merely a coincidence that he is gone too?"

"Alexio left for Siya because he could not wait for Aitnu's return with the news from Biyat. Your uncle told me this morning. I had no idea he was leaving. Since you seem unsettled by his mission, I assume you did not send him?"

"Of course not." With a nod to her husband, Pah accepted a leather pouch from him and put it in her lap. Unwrapping it with hurried fingers, she revealed what was inside.

"Nefret left this behind in Farrah's tent. I think this may have been the reason she killed her. Perhaps the

Old One caught her stealing this—I don't know, but I know my sister never owned such a thing."

The emerald and gold necklace fell into her lap and sparkled like a living thing. She picked it up and held it out to me as if it were a snake.

Blinking like a madman, I stammered, "Where did you get that?"

"I told you, Father. Nefret left this in Farrah's tent. The pouch was wrapped in one of her old tunics. She left some other things too, but this I do not recognize. I am sure it does not belong to her. Do you know where it came from? What is so special about it?"

Accepting the necklace from her, I squeezed it. "This necklace belonged to your mother and her mother before her. The last time I saw it, she was wearing it."

Pah rose from her chair, and her hand flew to her mouth. "How? How did Nefret get this?" Snatching the necklace back from me, she turned it over in her hand as if she would find the clues she was looking for written in the gold. There were letters on the back of the emerald pendant, but in a writing I could not understand. No one in the tribe could, except maybe Farrah. I missed the Old One already.

I had no answers and offered none.

"How do you know my mother had this necklace on when she disappeared? Perhaps she left it with Farrah? Or left it behind and the old woman hid it?"

I shrugged. "I can't know and neither can you, seeing as Farrah is dead now."

Yuni said, "It is the necklace of a queen. You should wear it, mekhma. It is yours by right." He offered to put it around her neck. I watched as she lifted her hair. The young man fastened the necklace, and she spun around so he could appraise her. "Almost as lovely as you, Pah."

She smiled, pleased with his comment. But her smile disappeared when she saw the look on my face. "You don't look pleased, Father. I suppose you are disappointed that I am the one wearing this necklace."

"No, I am remembering a dream I had last night. A warning dream, Pah. Your mother would not be happy—is not happy—that you and your sister have parted ways. She saw this. She saw all this the night you were born. She begged me to stop it, but I could not. I listened to the Council. I should have sent one of you away to Omel. Then I could have prevented this. You are strong together, Pah. You belong together, you and Nefret!"

She swung her thick gown behind her and flew toward me. "Now you say this? Now? What am I to think? It is too late to clear your conscience, Father. You made your choice, and you lost." The surprise must have shown on my face because she added with a smile, "Oh yes, I know all about it. You wanted Nefret as mekhma—this I know, but that is no matter now."

"I never wanted that. I did not want to follow the Old Ways!"

"Perhaps not, but here we are. I have won! I am mekhma! Take your regrets and leave, Father. I am relieving you of your duty." We stood eye to eye for an eternal moment. I raised my hand to plead sense with her, but she would not be swayed.

Yuni stood by her, his hand on her shoulder. "Send for your uncle. Perhaps he will be of better service to you." Pah agreed, and Yuni then left us alone.

My mind roiled with what I should say, what I should do. Kadeema's accusation rang in my ears: "What of our daughters, Semkah?" I would have to answer for my inaction one day. I had buried my heart in my own grief and had failed to protect them from Farrah's prophecy. I had failed.

Feeling an icy stare at my back, I walked out too.

Chapter Thirteen

Loving the Mekhma—Alexio

We heard them before we saw them. So ecstatic, so frenzied were they from their bloody victory that they did not notice us. There were only three of us, not enough to challenge the approaching horde. Phares was barely a man, and his brother Ohn was not much older. Still, they had been the only ones I could persuade to accompany me, and I refused to let Pah win the day. If I was going to sacrifice my life and my happiness for the tribe, it would mean something.

If I could have gone to Biyat to get proof of Nefret's testimony, then surely the Council would have reconsidered its decision. Unfortunately for me, I had not been selected for that mission. So my friends and I went in search of other proof that Nefret's warnings were real. If the threat was real, and I believed it was, our tribe was in danger. We could not afford to wait for Aitnu to return. He was traveling to all the tribes for an assessment. And the longer we waited to know the truth, the firmer the grip that Pah would have on the throne. Pah had stolen the throne from Nefret by refusing to wait for her to complete her task.

I had it on good authority that proof would force the Old Ones to weigh the trials anew. The whole clan needed Nefret—and I did not think that merely because I loved her more than my own heartbeat. I thought it because it was true. Nefret outshone her sister in many ways, especially in kindness, goodness and patience. No doubt Pah had courage, fierceness and strength, but she did not inspire me and would not hesitate in her ruthlessness.

No matter how many sweet words Pah whispered to me, no matter how like her sister she appeared in some ways, I could not give her what she wanted. In the end, I refused her, and it was then that she began her ruthless campaign against Nefret.

Now here I lay in the red sand on the side of a dune watching a black-cloaked band of murderers leaving the tiny oasis of Gemia, north of Timia. Tents burned, children screamed and goats shrieked as the bandits pierced them with spears. I grabbed Ohn's arm to prevent him from reaching for his bow. "There are too many, brother. We need to wait. Wait and watch. Be still, Ohn, Phares. Be still now." Ohn leaned against the dune and closed his eyes. Tears streamed down his young face.

"Yes, be still now. Our father will not be happy if I do not bring you home," Phares scolded his brother. Ohn obeyed and waited and watched until the raiding party left. They rode off into the distance without ever looking in our direction. They were not jinn or giants but men on a mission. I had seen my share of bloodthirstiness before, but these heinous acts were beyond anything I could have imagined. Children were decapitated, pregnant women had their bellies slit, and their unborn children emerged into the world in an untimely, bloody mess. The old men had their heads removed, but not before their eyes had been gouged out; their mouths gaped open in silent screams. Ohn vomited on his sandals and half the burnt grass of the oasis.

I had seen enough. There was no one alive, no one to testify against the killers. I wondered what I could bring back to the tribes to prove these tall men were indeed real and not a fabrication by a girl who had failed her trial and was desperate to claim the title of mekhma. I had no chance of following Aitnu or making it all the way to Biyat now. Perhaps if I had been by myself, but not with Phares and Ohn. Although brave and keen to serve with me, they did not have the stamina necessary to make such a speedy ride. I needed to go home; it was only a half day's ride back to Timia, too close to stand idly by and wait for the murderers to destroy our tribes. As I scanned the bloody scene, I wondered what proof to bring. Then I saw my answer. Pinned to the chest of a dead young man was a piece of fabric. Someone had taken the trouble to leave this message—it should not be ignored. I removed the sword from the dead boy's chest, saying a silent apology as I did, asking his forgiveness for this one last offense. I removed the cloth and shoved it into my tunic.

"Let us leave this place of death," I told the young men. Anxious to leave the horror behind us, we wasted no time. As swiftly as the animals would allow, we rode pell-mell to the east. I glanced behind me as we rode, trying to shake the feeling that the death god Osiris himself followed us.

I slapped the sides of the camel with my rough leather strap and hugged it, keeping my head down and back straight as I had been taught. Our tribe was known for its desert speed—proper riding technique was something the son of a king or even a half-king such as my father would be expected to know. Now I would put that talent to good use in the hope of saving my tribe and Nefret's. As I raced back toward Timia I prayed that all would be well with my people, although logic suggested that it would not be well at all. These tall men or whoever they were seemed to be specifically targeting Meshwesh. The Algat and other tribes were around, but no reports had come in from their locations. I had witnessed with my own eyes that these people had a bloodlust that knew no bounds.

Whoever they were, their reach was long, for they had traveled to Biyat and to the tiny oasis of Siya without much opposition. It only made sense that they would attack wealthy Timia, and in a way it was fortuitous that my father and his tribe were currently there. Together the tribes made a mighty force, but to withstand such a foe? We were not prepared! I needed the help of the entire clan! The Bee-Eater must be sent and the call made to all the Meshwesh. We would stand together, or we would die!

We crested a dune and suddenly Timia sprawled before us, lush, green and filled to the borders with Meshwesh warriors, their families and their lowing cattle. A heavy plunder waiting to be plucked. To my great relief all appeared safe. The camp was noisier than normal, but that was to be expected; the mekhma trials were historic events to even the lowliest Meshwesh. Representatives from some of the tribes had arrived to hear the decision of the Council; others had not made the trip. But there was not much argument. It had been accepted from their birth night that either Pah or Nefret would be the promised leader who would guide us back to Zerzura. One day we would be safe. Or so everyone assumed.

I pulled the reins of the camel and waved the brothers to me. "Listen to me. We don't have much time. Let me do the talking. I will find Semkah and give a report."

Ohn's eyes widened with surprise. "Yes, but the mekhma…." He appeared unsure. "Should we not speak to her first?"

"Please, you must trust me, brothers. I know what I am doing. Say nothing to anyone. Not yet."

Catching his breath after the furious ride, Phares nodded his consent, and together the three of us rode the rest of the way into camp. They busied themselves with the camels as I went in search of Semkah. From the moment I began to walk through the camp, I could feel the sadness. Something had happened! The faces of the Meshwesh were full of despair. I greeted many by name, but no one offered any explanation. Suddenly, women began to howl—and the hair on the back of my neck stood up. An urgency rose within me, and I ran faster toward the king's tent. What had happened?

Nefret!

I found Semkah in his tent with my father, in the midst of an argument. That was always the way with them, struggling with one another. My father's stubbornness and ambition made it difficult for him to trust anyone. For my uncle's part, he kept his involvement to a minimum, leaving many to believe that he was not confrontational enough to be the clan's warrior-king. I knew firsthand that it was a title that father coveted. Theirs was a difficult relationship to manage, and few tried to interfere.

"What has happened?" I blurted out, trying to catch my breath.

"Foolish boy! What do you mean by leaving without my permission! You know we planned to leave today and now… "

"Farrah is dead," my uncle broke in.

"What? How?" Again the hair on my neck crinkled.

"That is what we must find out, but you must account for yourself." Father's dark brows knitted together.

"I have the proof—Nefret told the truth. Don't you want to know the truth? Look at this! It was found on the body of a dead boy at Gemia. All of them are dead! Just like Biyat and Siya! This is the proof that it was as she says." I pulled the bloody rag out of my tunic and handed it to the king. Without a word, Semkah took it.

"You say you found this at Gemia?" he asked as he spread the crumpled cloth out on the table.

"Yes, uncle."

"The raiders are moving." Semkah's voice shook.

"Yes, my king. The Meshwesh at Gemia were all dead. We saw them—the tall men. One of them pinned this to a man with the man's own blade."

My father made a snorting sound. "We have no king anymore, boy. We have a mekhma, remember? What happens if she finds out you left without permission?"

Defiantly I challenged him. "I am no boy. Uncle, Father, surely this symbol means something. A message, perhaps?"

"More like a warning," Semkah said. He leaned over a lambskin map that rested perpetually on a sturdy table with an onyx top.

Together the three of us stared at the map and then the cloth, but the pattern was not clear to me. After a moment, Semkah turned the cloth and the image became apparent. A lightning bolt clutched in a hand.

"What is this? What does it mean?"

"I have seen this before, Omel. This is Kiffian. The hand symbol—these are the tall men. We thought they were all dead."

"I have seen them, my king. They are indeed tall—taller than any Meshwesh. And they kill without mercy. No one will stand before them if we do not prepare for battle. I have no doubt they will come here next. Why wouldn't they?"

"You should leave the battle planning to us, boy."

"Father, this is…"

Before we could continue, a great commotion filled the camp. The mourning wails were replaced with screams of terror. We raced outside to see with our own eyes what we already knew. The tall men had arrived—they must have followed us here!

"By the gods! We must fight!" I ran behind them toward the racks that held our wicker shields and curved fighting blades, and my father raced before us all.

Semkah reached for me. "Wait! You must find Nefret!"

"Where is she?"

"She left this morning. Look to the north; she headed to Petra."

"But why? Why would she go there?"

"Because I sent her! I let this happen. I have no right to ask, but please help her. Go now—go north. She cannot be that far ahead."

The shrill sounds of swords clashing and screams filled the air. I caught a glimpse of Phares and Ohn, who ran into the fray with their swords drawn and were battling clumsily for their lives. The invaders were tall and muscular—much taller than the slender Meshwesh. Semkah towered over most of his tribe, and even the king was slight in comparison to the red-haired Kiffians. I watched my father run toward a massive beast of a man and with one swing cut the man down. Swords clanged, and the Kiffians pressed into the camp easily, killing all who tried to stand against them.

"But I must fight! You need me!" I screamed at him, still ready to race into battle. "Ohn!"

I saw Ohn fall to the ground not fifty feet away, and blood gurgled from his mouth. A giant laughed above him, ignoring his pleas for mercy. I lurched toward him, but Semkah grasped my arm.

"Please, for the love you bear my daughter! Go! While you still can!" Then the angry king turned on his heel and pulled his curved blade from his belt. With a war cry, Semkah spun and lunged toward the nearest enemy. His blow landed perfectly at the beast's neck.

With a heart torn in two, I ran back toward the nearest camel—I could not linger if I was to obey Semkah. I reasoned with myself that I was merely following the king's commands, not abandoning my brothers or my father. As if he could read my mind, Father called me. His sword banged another and he struggled with his foe. "Alexio! Come now, son! Help us!"

With all my heart I wanted to heed his summons, but I had to find Nefret. Surely he would understand. With the sounds of war in my ears, I rode away as tears streaked my face. Once more I heard someone call my name. I did not look back.

I knew it was a sound that I would never forget.

Chapter Fourteen

For the Tribe—Nefret

The North Star shone bright when I left Timia. I followed it obediently, reminding myself of my father's promise to help me. I was not alone. I followed the star until the sun rose and then kept my path straight toward the north and to Petra.

Farrah had taught us that Petra was haunted, and now here I was racing toward that very place. According to my father it would take five days to reach Petra, but what would I find there if and when I made it? Probably no living soul. I shuddered under my cloak thinking of the story of Numa and the jinn. I had never heard of the Nabataeans until I was sent to their court.

All that we knew—all that we had been told—was a lie. I had seen the Shining Man; he made no claim to be a god, yet I knew he was something other than human. And he was in control of my life. Besides him, there were no gods and goddesses. Isis, Hathor even our dead ancestors—they could not hear the voices of mere mortals. No one cared for man, only men themselves. I struggled with this new realization and thought of my sister, who now ruled our tribe. I had been wise to leave, of that much I was sure. No doubt she would've made an example of me, parading me in front of her friends before she sent me to my death in the desert with no water or food or even the companionship of a donkey or camel.

Poor Paimu! Whenever she came out of hiding, how angry she would be to know that I left without her. *Forgive me, little one.*

How strange it was to see no one. Every morning before, I had been met with friendly Meshwesh faces. Isha, who gave me bread. Paimu and Ziza, who chattered through their breakfast nearly every sunrise. Now I was doomed to a life without the company of my clan. Why had Father sent me here? There were no Meshwesh in Petra. Was I to remain by myself? Surrounded by a sea of sadness, I continued to track north. I spied a few serpents and caught a glimpse of a clever hawk searching for those slithering tasty morsels. They quickly hid themselves in the sand. I was like them now, a lowly snake hiding in the sand. Tears welled up in my eyes but I did not allow myself the luxury of crying. I needed to preserve my water, not shed it over my heartless sister.

Soon the heat of the day was upon me, and I began to worry about where I would find shelter from the blazing hot afternoon. To add to my discomfort, the wind began to blow, kicking up sand all around me. Wrapping the cloak around my face, I made a slit for my eyes and continuously scanned the horizon for a place to camp.

Someone must be looking out for me, I thought, as just a few minutes later I spotted a rocky outcropping nearby. I made for it quickly but cautiously, knowing I may not be the only person looking for shelter. Sweating under my cloak, I dismounted from my camel and led him up the side of the rocky hill. He complained and spat furiously, but I was immune to his disdain. "I am trying to save our lives, stupid," I scolded him. Clucking at him, I snapped the rein a few times, and he unhappily followed me. "Just a little further—come on now. I will call you Ginku, the stubborn one." He snorted his disapproval but obeyed me.

We inched upwards until we came to the flat place. "Here we go. This will do. You sit there." I patted his shoulder and immediately he plunked down, curling his legs under him. In just a few minutes I had a makeshift shelter made of a cloth and two sticks I had carried with me from Timia. Unrolling my bedroll, I sat upon the pallet, happy to be off the swaying camel for a little while. The sun burned above me, but my small patch of shade brought some relief. I took a long drink from my goatskin.

I had been riding for hours—at least six, but it felt longer. Every step away from my tribe was a step toward the unknown. I was too tired to build a fire for food. I looked around nervously, hoping there were no bandits secreted in the caves above me. Even in the land of the Meshwesh it would be foolish to believe that a single woman was safe here among the many peoples of the desert. To the untrained eye, the Red Sands may have seemed like an endless sea. But to the intrepid trader or mercenary, the Sahara was a highway—a rich highway loaded with treasures, including slaves.

For the first time in my life, I whispered a prayer into the surrounding heat. I had no incense, no gifts or food to offer, only my words. "If you can hear me, I beg you. Lead me as you promised you would."

With sleepy eyes but an active mind, I forced my eyes to remain closed.

Suddenly I was flying, soaring above the reddish-brown earth below me. I was no longer Nefret but a falcon—a Heret falcon with massive, curved wings. With just a flick of my wings I rose high, soaring on the gust into the white clouds. With an easy flutter, I sailed downward and began to skim the sands. I screeched and rose higher and higher until again the lands below appeared small and unimportant. From my cloudy hiding place, I watched and waited. But for what I did not know.

Then like a massive snake, a band of tall men on dark-haired camels raced across the desert in perfect formation. The camels were hunkered low as the riders slapped them ruthlessly to run faster and faster. I swooped down to get a closer look at the tall men's faces. Their hands were bloody, evidence of a recent assault. Their black clothing was stained with rust-colored blood. They let out a gleeful shout as they sailed across the sands, happy that they had accomplished their evil deed. I dove even closer to get a look at what bounty they carried away. With my excellent falcon vision, I detected living beings.

Thrown across the saddle of the leader, in a crumpled heap of copper hair and torn clothing, was my sister. An evil gash stretched down her bloody arm, which hung motionless from her side. With her other arm she clutched her ripped gown to cover her naked breasts. I dove down further until I flew beside the giants and was even with Pah. Panicked, I called her name, but all that emerged from my lips was an ear-splitting screech. Pah's fevered eyes opened, and she looked at me with anguish and regret.

"Sister!" she cried out, reaching for me with her good hand.

Suddenly the scene changed—I was no longer a falcon.

I cried out to her again, "Pah!" She was gone, her face disappearing like someone wiped their hand across a pool of water.

I stood in an empty valley. I wore warrior's clothing, a leather vest and armbands, with my quiver on my back. Standing upon a high hill, I watched the horizon and waited for our enemy to approach. Below me were the Meshwesh, few in number but fearlessly ready for battle. They gazed up at me and began to sing the song of Zerzura. I raised my arms high and sang it with them.

> *We are the children of the Red Lands*
> *We are the children of Ma'at*
> *Zerzura, Zerzura, let us come home to you*
> *For our blood is your blood, our land is your land*
> *Zerzura, Zerzura, we come home to you...*

On the horizon I saw the tall men approach on their black camels. They were greater in number this time, with a determined look of absolute hatred upon their faces. In that moment, it was as if I could read their hearts and see their thoughts. It was the gold they were after, the gold and the turquoise, and our children and anything of value. There was no mercy in them. In the valley below me I watched an extraordinary sight—a whistle blew, and the Meshwesh retreated into their secret places. They hid under the ground in hollowed-out holes that were covered with grass and branches. In their hands were their curved blades, sharpened savagely and poised for attack. Some had even taken the trouble of wetting the blades' edges with poison so that even the most glancing of cuts would be lethal. My heart swelled with pride. I alone stood on the hill above them, a gold shield in my hand. I turned the shield to catch the sun. It glinted, beckoning the Kiffians toward me and to their fate. Again I could read the minds and the hearts of the approaching horde. "We have them surrounded!" I laughed at them as they ran to their doom. The faces of the dead flashed before me, and I awoke screaming.

Alexio's handsome face hovered over me. "Nefret!"

"Alexio? Am I dreaming still?"

His beautiful smile told me that I was not. I threw my arms around him and held him close. I kissed his cheek and touched his face, hair and arms. "You *are* here. You are not a dream."

"No, I am not," he said gently. "Your father sent me to find you. The camp is under attack, Nefret. The tall men are Kiffians. They are the ones you saw—I am sure of it. They have murdered everyone at Biyat, Siya and Gemia, and I fear for those at Timia. Even with our numbers we are outmatched and were overtaken quickly. I do fear the worst."

He appraised our surroundings. "This is not a safe place. We must go higher."

"What do you mean? We must go back! Our people need us."

"We cannot help them. I have to protect you, princess. The king ordered me to do so."

"Stop calling me that. I am no princess. I am an outcast, remember? I'm nobody."

Walking toward me in angry strides, Alexio said, "And yet you want to go back for them? Stop this foolish talk. We do not have time for it. We cannot go back right now, but we will go back. We must be smart and wait a while. Trust me when I say to you there's nothing you can do for our people now. But they will need you when the battle is over."

"How can you ask me to sit here and wait? They have taken my sister—I have seen it!"

Alexio pushed his hair out of his eyes and stared at me. "What do you mean you have seen it?"

"I saw it in a dream. I know it sounds crazy—I sound like Farrah—but I did see it! They have Pah, and I must get her back."

His face crumpled at the mention of the Old One. "Farrah is dead now. She has died."

"What?"

"And there is more. I don't know how else to tell you this. Paimu—she is dead too. Both were stabbed and buried in the sand. Before you jump to your sister's side, you should know that she implicated you in these crimes. In fact my father and yours were in the midst of an argument over what to do about all this when the enemy rode in."

"She would never—how could she dream that I would do that! Oh gods, not my treasure! Not my heart! Paimu!" I crumpled under the weight of the shocking news. Alexio caught me, and I freely wept for the sweet little girl I had left behind.

Never again would I see her climb a tree or hear her count my silver bracelets.

My heart! I should never have left you, little one! I am so sorry…

After a few minutes of silence, Alexio said softly, "We must go higher; we must find shelter. The Kiffians rode in from the west—I suspect that they will ride south with…their plunder, but we cannot be sure. Who knows? I do know that you and I are no match for the dozens of warriors that fell on Timia. We need to hide. I think I see a cave opening just there. Do you see it?"

I pretended to glance up but saw nothing beyond the wall of red rocks. I nodded.

"Can you make it?"

"Of course," I said woodenly.

With a broken heart I did as Alexio asked. I packed my makeshift tent quickly and followed him up the ragged wall of red. The path to the top was narrow—we left our camels below, but unless someone climbed up, they would not see them.

Alexio scampered ahead of me and thoroughly searched the cave for animals. It would not be unusual to find a desert cat or a nest of snakes hiding in the cool dampness of the cave. Finding shelter from the heat was the priority of every living creature. Fortunately, there were none, only a few dried snakeskins, and we moved in. Alexio made our beds, and I dug through my bag for food. I suspected he had nothing to eat since he left camp so quickly, and I knew he would be hungry. For me, I did not think I would ever eat again. Paimu's trusting face haunted me. I could not fathom who could take her life so callously. No life for Paimu. Her murder took not only her life but also the lives of her children.

Pah! How could you?

If she had done this thing, she would pay for her crime, I vowed.

Alexio prepared his weapons and slid a blade under his blanket. I wondered what he was thinking. That this was my fault? That he should be with his tribe and his father fighting our enemies? I wondered why my father would send him to me.

I shared my bread and water with Alexio, and we hunkered down to wait out the sun. We had a long wait ahead of us; both of us sat in silence wondering what had happened to our loved ones. It was bad enough that Paimu and Farrah were dead, but the truth was that many more would likely die today.

"What do you think we will find when we go back, Alexio? Will there be anyone left? And where shall we go? We cannot go to Biyat or Siya. The only place I can think of is north to Petra. My father told me to go see the Nabataeans. We need help, someone to stand with us. Maybe the Algeans. They're always hungry for our gold. What do you know of our allies?"

"I think we are on our own, Nefret. The Cushites would never stand against the Kiffians—neither would the Algeans. Besides, the Algeans have all moved to the west." His dark eyes appraised me, and he rubbed his hands through his dark curls. "There is only one ally I can think of that would help us; only one that would have the strength to hit these Kiffians with a heavy hand. They could crush them!"

"You mean Egypt?"

"Yes."

"You sound just like your father," I said contemptuously. Just the idea of begging Egypt for help made my blood boil. I had heard this argument many times between my uncle and my father. "You know what will happen if we go to Egypt. They will take our gold—they will take everything. We will be slaves, Alexio."

"Now you sound like *your* father. What choice do we have? Who cares about the gold and the turquoise if we have no blood in our bodies? Who cares about any of this if we have no life? I would not rule anything out at this point."

I leaned against the dry cavern wall and stared at him in the dim light. I sighed and said, "Yes, you're probably right. And we know nothing and will know nothing until we return to Timia." A ragged sigh escaped from deep within my soul. "Now would be a good time for the gods to show us the way back to Zerzura. With Farrah's death, I wonder if we shall ever know."

He lay on his pallet and stared at the cave's ceiling. "She did not know, Nefret. She forgot the way, and you know that. We should rest. If we get up early, we can make our way back and no one will see us—unless we want them to."

"Very well." I lay down too, but my mind would not stop speaking. I agonized over my lost Paimu.

Despite the blazing heat outside, the cave felt cool and comfortable. Eventually I dozed. We would have a long ride back to Timia. Alexio fell asleep quickly, and his light snoring comforted me. It was funny to think that just an hour ago I believed I would live as a hermit, a forgotten one lost in the dead city of Petra. I had not yet made up my mind as to whether I would contact the Nabataean king or not. That was before. Now, I was not alone. How quickly fate changed her mind about me!

I frowned into the dimness. Did I want to return to the people who rejected me? Well, it had been my choice to leave without their blessing. Perhaps if I had stayed, things would have been different.

"Not with Pah," my own voice whispered in my head.

I fell asleep but did not dream. My body was tired, my legs sore. It felt good to sleep without fear. Suddenly I was awake—the cave was freezing, and darkness covered the desert sands. The cold threatened to creep into my bones, and I quickly scampered about the mouth of the cave looking for anything I could burn. A small fire would warm us until it was time to ride.

After I arranged the small pile of debris I found, I cracked my fire stones together to create the sparks. Finally a small blaze began, and I warmed my hands.

"What are you doing?" Alexio tossed handfuls of sand onto my fire.

I gasped in surprise and stared at him with my hand on my hip. "What did you do that for? I am freezing!"

"Do you want to draw attention to us? Then set the cave on fire if you like. I am sure some Kiffian would be happy to take you as his wife."

I gasped at his rudeness, but he did not say more. He quickly surveyed the horizon, returned to his bed and rolled his cover around his body. He was determined to ignore me, but I was still cold. And now I was angry too. I crept to the mouth of the cave to peer outside and saw nothing but darkness. I listened and heard nothing. He was right. How foolish I had been to do such a thing! How would I ever survive on my own? I shivered, wrapping my cloak around me.

"If you are cold, lie next to me. Just don't set me on fire."

I snorted at his comment but made my way to his pallet. My teeth were chattering now, and my sandals offered my toes no warmth. Awkwardly, I dragged my pallet next to his and curled up to his back, my face pressed against him. Still shivering, I enjoyed the warmth. He reached behind his back and offered me his hand. I took it, and he rubbed the back of my hand absently until the warmth returned. Then I wrapped my arm around his. He tossed his blanket around me, and I cuddled closer. Now warm and comfortable, I still could not sleep. Despite the sadness of the day, I was very much aware that I was lying next to the man I loved.

Chapter Fifteen

The Red Sands—Nefret

The ride back to Timia seemed to last a lifetime, but time seemed even slower when we arrived there. Over half of our tribes had either bled out in the sands or perished by Kiffian blades. After a tour of the remains of our camp, it was apparent to Alexio, Orba and me that we had to move quickly. They had not finished their destruction, for some of us yet lived. Our enemies could return at any time, and with our injured we would not survive another assault. Many of our animals had perished, and others had been stolen, including our camels—the only ones that were left were crippled or otherwise harmed. Like most of the Meshwesh, the remaining camels could not endure a long trek across the hot desert. Wherever we went, it had to be close.

My uncle decided to ride home to Fayyum, gather reinforcements and return to us. It would be a day's wait, but if the gods favored us, we would have the time we needed to care for our injured. As I walked through the camp sharing water from my goatskin and distributing any food that we could scrounge, I made a mental list of the fallen. Ayn's parents died in the assault as well as Ziza and her family. We discreetly buried our dead, but I gave strict orders that no warning or lamentation would be offered for our lost ones. We could not risk the sounds attracting the Kiffians or any other traitor who might take advantage of our tragedy. I assured them we would mourn at the appropriate time.

Mina cared for my father night and day. The older woman did not speak, but an endless stream of tears flowed from her eyes. When first she saw me she grasped me as a drowning man would seize the one who came to save him. She collapsed on me, her silent sobs shaking her body violently. At first I thought she herself had been wounded, for she was covered in blood, but after an examination I could see she was not. Undoubtedly, Farrah's acolyte wore the blood of those she had tried to save.

"What happened to Farrah and Paimu, Mina? Can't you tell me?"

She looked at her dirty hands and shook her head slowly. I took her face in my hands and could see the anguish in her eyes.

"What about Pah? Did you see my sister?"

Mina's eyes widened, but she kept her silence. If I was to know what had happened to any of them, I would have to find another source of information. I resisted the urge to express my frustration in a way that would harm Mina. She had been through enough. Forcing her to break her vow of silence would not help heal us.

"It is all right, Mina. Thank you for all you have done."

She made the sign of respect and backed away from me, presumably to return to caring for my father. He had not yet recovered—his right arm had been so viciously sliced that it had to be removed. It had hung by a few pieces of skin and threatened to rot and take his life. I visited him many times a day to check on his progress but always left disappointed. He had not stirred or opened his eyes since he had fallen.

Alexio had been my constant companion. He helped me reorganize the camp, collect any weapons we could scavenge and distribute the food. I honestly did not know how I would have survived without his help. The day of waiting for Omel to return drove me mad. I passed the time wiping away blood and tears and spent any stolen moments I could wondering about my sister's fate. As night fell, I studied the stars, hoping to find a clue, but saw nothing. The people began to openly call me mekhma, and I did not dissuade them. They needed something to believe in, and I would be that rallying point, at least until my sister could be recovered.

Alexio and Orba sat with me, and we discussed our next steps. We would have to move slowly, so the plan was to flee to the rocky outcropping where Alexio and I had spent the night. We believed there were enough caves to keep us safe. From there, we would go north, presumably to Petra. I didn't like the plan, but it was as good as any I could think of.

As difficult as it was to believe, we could very easily disappear into the Sahara and never be seen again, or missed.

When Orba left us, Alexio and I sat quietly with our minds racing. This seemed more and more like an impossible task, yet we never expressed our doubt. We had to live! Although our enemy had stolen our precious treasures, our children, and murdered many of our warriors, they had left us water. Omel would return to the camp in the morning, if all went as planned. I did not even want to think about the possibility that he might abandon us. Surely he would not!

Alexio and I would have only this one last night together. I felt guilty for the thoughts I had about my cousin. All around us were the signs of death. Yet in my heart I thought of nothing but Alexio. I knew he was thinking the same thing, for at every turn I found his eyes upon me, searching me; his desire for me was obvious even to me, an inexperienced young woman.

Late that night, when the camp became quiet, Alexio and I found ourselves at the pool of Timia. We had not planned such a rendezvous, at least neither of us spoke of it, but there we were. Together at last. On my order, the camp was dark except for a few small fires used to cook and offer some light; soon even those would be put out. The moon hid itself behind rare clouds, like the gods themselves hid us from our enemies. It rarely rained in the desert—some people could go a lifetime and not see rain—but I could smell the rain in the air. Farrah once told me that whenever you smelled the rain it was a sign.

Good things always happened when it rained.

As if it were the most natural thing in the world, we removed our clothing just as we had when we were children. Without timidity we slipped quietly into the pool. There was no giggling, no splashing, no children's jokes. We swam close to one another, not talking or smiling. Suddenly, Alexio stood up in the water, and his wet, muscular figure gleamed in the moonlight. He offered his hand to me and I accepted it, rising and slinging water from my hair. There was no space between us. I felt the strength of his body pressed against mine, the shocking hardness of him. I felt soft and small but unafraid. We stood together, our bodies pressed up against one another, and we kissed unashamedly. I felt no guilt that Alexio had once been promised to another, for I knew that girl was gone. I had helped bury her. In all the world, at least in that moment, there was only Alexio and me.

The date palms beside us swayed under the influence of the winds. I half wondered if we were responsible for this storm, our passion suppressed for so long now that it had loosed the elements themselves. We kissed again; neither of us spoke. He took my hand, not bothering to dress. I reached for my tunic and covered my naked body with it, following him into the darkness just beyond the camp.

We were alone at last with no lights in sight. It felt like we were the only people in the world. Rain sprinkled down upon us like an anointing from above. In the rain there was a solemnity, and I was very aware that what we were about to do was not unseen by the gods or our ancestors. I wondered what Farrah would say about our union.

I held Alexio's hands in my own and kissed them. His beautiful dark face radiated a complex blend of desire and seriousness.

"Are you sure you want to do this?" he asked, his voice rough and needy.

"Yes, I am sure." I drew myself up tall and straight as I had seen Farrah do and said, "I am the Queen of the Meshwesh. I take you, Alexio hap Omel, as my consort. From this day forward you are my equal. Hear me, oh gods and ancestors, this is my husband, the one I choose. Bind us together for eternity. Bind us together, body, soul and mind. For we are one."

Alexio's brilliant smile flashed across his face. He repeated my words. "Hear me, oh gods and ancestors, this is my wife, the one I choose. Bind us together for eternity. Bind us together, body, soul and mind. For we are one."

We fell to our knees, and the weightiness of what we had just done surprised me.

With the formalities completed, Alexio and I lost ourselves in one another's arms. He was gentle and kind at first, stroking my skin, touching my hair, kissing my lips. Yet that was not enough for me—I wanted more of him, not to be toyed with. I needed him as a woman needs a man.

With rising urgency, I wrapped my arms around him and pulled him close to me. I knew enough about lovemaking to know that it could be painful, but I welcomed the pain. I who had suffered so little compared to my people deserved to feel pain. I wanted this. I demanded it.

Fiercely I whispered, "Do not be easy, Alexio."

My words made him shudder, and he obeyed me. I kept my eyes trained on his handsome face. I slid my arms under his shoulders and pushed my body against his. He responded, penetrating me quickly as I had asked him to do. I cried out in pain as I felt my maidenhead burn away. It was a sacrifice to the Sahara, a blood covenant between Alexio and me. As the pain subsided, other sensations crept over me; a surprising warmth emanated from all parts of my body. For a moment, we hung there together in our pleasure before he collapsed beside me on the sand.

When it was over, he kissed my neck and stroked my copper hair. I shed no tears. I felt no shame. What we had done was right. It was the beginning of healing for our tribes. According to the Old Ways, our union made us father and mother of Meshwesh. I had been the mekhma, the mother of our clan. Now the clan had a father as well.

We rose from the sand no longer Nefret and Alexio. We were one.

And we would always be together!

Chapter Sixteen

Astora's Eyes—Omel

Astora greeted me with her lovely smile, but the sight saddened my soul. She looked beyond me, expecting to see her son riding behind me, but she would not see him. Never again. Her queen's blue jewel dangled upon her pretty brow and sparkled in the light. Upon closer inspection, the woman whimpered at my appearance.

"Omel? Is that blood? Are you injured? Where is Suri?" Others surrounded me, curious to hear the fate of the young man. "Suri!" she called.

"Cut down. Kiffians overran Biyat, Siya, Gemia and Timia. The tribes at Biyat and Siya have been murdered, but there are a few that remain at Timia. We must go to them. Benada! Omri! Gather supplies and men. We ride for Timia within the hour!"

"Kiffians? How long has it been?" Omri asked, the young man's eyes narrow and angry.

"I will go gather what we need," Benada answered, taking Omri with him.

"Suri?" Astora asked again.

"It is true, Astora. He is gone, but Suri fought bravely," I lied.

The image of the boy pinned to the ground by a Kiffian's blade appeared unsummoned in my mind. It was I who had cut Suri's attacker down, first sliding my blade across the back of his knees. Then, spinning like an angry whirlwind, I had removed his screaming head from his shoulders. In a final act of defiance, the severed head had rolled onto Suri's convulsing body.

With a vicious kick I had sent it skittering across the grass and with an anguished cry pulled the weapon from the skinny boy's stomach. His mouth had spewed crimson, and his dark, frightened eyes pleaded for help but only for a moment. I squatted beside him, whispering the words I had never spoken during his life, "My son." He made an inaudible gurgling sound and left this world's realm.

But this I would never tell his mother. Nor would I tell of Alexio's desertion—how he left me and his brother and fled into the desert. I spat on the ground at the memory. She hated him for reasons I never understood.

Astora buried her face in my chest, and I stroked her hair gingerly. Perhaps I could have delivered the news differently, but there was no time to navigate feelings. I did not cry, although sorrow pierced my heart as well. I could not allow myself the luxury of tears when our lives were hanging in the balance. I would mourn Suri in my own way when the time was right.

"Astora, listen to me. You must gather everything you can—we have to move. It is not safe to stay here. We must gather together all the Meshwesh if we are to stand against these invaders." Her eyes were full of questions, and tears streamed down her dusky face. "No, you must trust me. We will mourn our son, but now we must go. Pack the oils, and we will bury him together. Do you understand?"

She nodded and then examined my face with narrowed eyes. "What of Alexio? Is he dead also?"

"No. Hurry now. You must lead the women. We leave within the hour." Something passed behind her eyes, but I could not fathom it. One day I would get to the bottom of her hatred for my eldest son, but today was not that day.

Chapter Seventeen

The Unseen Hand—Nefret

My uncle had returned—I heard the sounds of jubilation, but I did not join in the welcoming party. Our relationship had always been distant. I had the distinct impression that Omel disapproved of me in some important way. Perhaps because he and Father were always at odds or because Pah went out of her way to endear herself to him. It was not until the trials that I saw clearly how much he favored her. But now she was gone. Grief stabbed in my heart. No, I would not give up on her. Somehow I would find her.

Father stirred beside me. I press the cloth against his feverish forehead. His eyes flickered open, "Kadeema."

"No, Father. It is me—Nefret."

"Nefret." Recognition flickered across his face, and he gave a ragged sigh.

"Do you want some water?" I filled the sponge with water and pressed it against his lips. He pulled the water from the sponge thirstily. I smiled at him. Surely this was a good sign.

"My arm?"

My smile disappeared. I did not want to tell this warrior that he was a warrior no longer, but what else could I do? "It is gone, Father. Orba did all he could to save it." Despite the removal of the nearly severed arm, the chance of infection and death remained. The stitches were red, and Orba had gone in search of the ingredients he needed to cleanse and fuse the wound. Father attempted to move his shoulder but grimaced in pain. His tanned skin was pale—his dark eyes stared at the white canvas that hung above him as he gasped.

"In my tunic pocket—the necklace. Take it."

As I removed the necklace from his bloodstained tunic, my breath caught in my throat. I had forgotten about my found prize. The green stones felt cool in my hand.

"Where did you find this?" he asked me.

"I found it in the sand behind the camp. I know that it is forbidden to leave the oasis unattended, but I needed time to myself. I am sorry, Father."

His head rolled with a halfhearted laugh. "You have no need to apologize. You are the mekhma—you always were. I told those fools! The necklace proves that."

"What does the necklace have to do with the mekhma?"

"It was Kadeema's necklace."

I sat still, trying to comprehend his words. Surely these were the words of a fevered brain. "How can that be?"

He shook his head sadly. "It is not by chance that you found this. Your mother led you to it. Claim it and keep it, Nefret. It is a queen's necklace—it belongs to the queens of Grecia whose blood runs in your veins. Now you are truly the queen of the Meshwesh."

Clutching the necklace tightly, I whispered, "My mother's necklace. I have heard the story of her disappearance, but I know nothing about her. You never speak of her." I did not mean to upbraid him at such a time, but to hear him speak of such things was a rare event. Perhaps it was the fever after all.

"Wear it. Put it on and claim your right."

With shaking fingers I did as he asked me. His warm hand cupped my face, and he gazed into my eyes. "There is much you do not know. I have not been a good father."

"You are the best of fathers!" I held his hand and squeezed it.

"A nice lie. Such love—love that I do not deserve. So like your mother. All these years I believed she left me. I wanted to believe that. In that there was at least some peace." Tears slid down his temples. "I should have known she would never have left me or our daughters." I could hear my uncle and the men of Fayyum, my uncle's tribe, approaching.

"Promise me something."

"Yes. Anything, Father."

"Find your sister. Whatever her crimes, she does not deserve such a fate."

"I will find her—I promise." With a groan of pain, he lay still with his eyes clamped closed.

I mulled over his words, hoping he would sleep. But with sudden ferocity his eyes sprang open and he said, "Omel will say that you are too young to lead—too inexperienced—but do not listen. If you renounce your right to rule, even temporarily, you will never get it back. He is not an evil man, but he is stubborn and ambitious, and these are troubling times."

"Yes, Father."

"Nefret, you must rally the remaining tribes. Go to Saqqara and tell the tribes to meet you there. If Biyat and Siya have fallen, the only place you can go is east."

"But what about the Nabataeans?"

"No, stay away from Petra now. You must go to Saqqara! Have Farrah…no, I forgot. Have Orba send the sigil of the Bee-Eater to all of the remaining tribes. They will answer; they will obey. Go to Saqqara. The Kiffians will not follow you there—it is the City of the Dead. They fear it." Bright red color bled through the bandages that Orba had encircled his stump with.

"Father, your wound! Hold still until Orba returns. We can discuss this later."

"There is no time! Listen to me."

"Yes, Father."

"Egypt is the answer."

"Egypt? What about the Cushites or the Algat? Haven't you said all your life that we cannot trust Egypt?"

"The Kiffians will come again. This time they'll come with fire and they'll burn everything away. There will be nothing left. Go to Egypt, to Pharaoh. He knows the way to Zerzura. You must unite the clan—take us home, Nefret." He groaned in pain, and sweat poured off his forehead.

The snakes of destiny twisted in my stomach. My father had been a wise ruler, and I knew he offered me his best advice.

"Go now. Meet Omel. Do not let him see me like this. Be strong and don't waver. You must build the tribe's confidence—give them something to believe in, Nefret. You can do this."

I kissed his forehead and stood on shaky legs. Thirsty and exhausted, I straightened my clothes and opened my tunic slightly so all would see my necklace clearly. The necklace would be proof to them that I was doubly a queen. I would let no man challenge me. With my head held high, I stepped out from under the canvas. With a purposeful stride, I went to meet my uncle and his tribe.

My uncle and his consort were busy greeting and consoling my people. An old woman wept upon Astora's shoulder, and Astora whispered in her ear. Since my uncle did not greet me as I approached, I called out to him. Without summoning them, Ayn and Alexio took their places beside me; one on my left and the other on my right. I did not look at them, but their presence gave me strength.

"Omel, thank you for returning so swiftly. My people thank you." Omel did not make haste to greet me, but he did not risk ignoring me either. He bowed briefly and summoned his consort to attend me. My father had been right. Omel had a mind to rule. Astora walked toward me with her arms wide open. A look of understanding and sadness was upon her face, but it was merely a mask. Her expressive black eyes revealed something very different. I stepped back from her arms, refusing her embrace, and greeted her with respect.

"Astora, I welcome you to Timia. Your healing hands are welcome here, for there is much to do before we leave in the morning." My words grabbed my uncle's attention, and he faced me now. His expression was angry, even aggravated.

"Go? Where are we going?"

"We leave Timia in the morning before the sun casts its first light over the desert." I looked him steadily in the eyes. He wanted to say something, but I rebuffed him. I turned to face the tribe that was gathering around us. I felt such sympathy for them. Broken, confused and without hope. These were my people!

Once again I felt the unseen hand moving across my heart and mind. In the crowd, I imagined the Shining Man smiling and watching me. It gave me confidence to believe that the words I was about to speak were his words. Indeed, I believed that they were. I raised my voice as I had heard Farrah do a hundred times before. I missed the Old One, but I continued in my speech.

"Sons and daughters of Ma! It is true that Biyat, Siya and Gemia have been overrun! It is true that many of our brothers and sisters here at Timia have vanished from the earth and will never walk in the Land of the Living again. But it is also true that we are alive and that their blood and the blood of our ancestors still flows in our veins. We can no longer be many tribes; we must be one clan! We are Meshwesh!"

Some of the women cried, and I could not help but notice that there were very few children among us. *Oh, Paimu!* Still, many were stirred by my words and shouted, "Hafa-nu, mekhma!" It was a phrase that meant much, both an expression of thanks and an offering of blessing. I raised my hand in acknowledgment and continued.

"These are evil days. Many of us have lost much. Even our mekhma, my own sister, has fallen prey to these evil men. But they shall not prevail. Tomorrow we leave for Saqqara. It is many days' walk to reach the City of the Dead, but we shall be safe there."

Astora scoffed. "Saqqara? What will we do there? There are no oases, and the Egyptians will not welcome us into their territory. Are we to dig graves and become one with those who have been buried in the brick mountains?" She sneered at me. Ayn hissed at her, but I ignored her.

"As mekhma, I will send the sigil of the Bee-Eaters to the remaining tribes, summoning them to Saqqara. I need riders to carry the sigils. Who will ride for me?" Many men volunteered, even my uncle, but I could not risk an insurrection. If my uncle were to rally another tribe against me, it would mean further division and death for the Meshwesh.

"Brave uncle, you honor me with your hand, but I need you here as a valued member of my Council. You men—yes, you four. You must leave with all haste and return to us at Saqqara. Ayn!"

"Yes, mekhma?"

"Take these men to Orba. He will find the sigils. Provide them with everything they need for their journey." With the sign of respect, Ayn backed away and did as I bade her. The men followed close behind her. Alexio and I stood together—I resisted the urge to reach out and take his hand. This was no time to show weakness.

"Tonight there will be no fires. If you must cook, prepare what you need now. When darkness falls upon the Red Lands, let everything be silent. No songs. No mourning. Keep quiet. Mothers, tend to your babies. We will not fall prey to this enemy again. The darkness will protect us. My uncle will assign warriors to watch the camp through the night." Omel stared at me but did not argue. "You will go to the caves and then on to Saqqara. It is a long journey. Pack wisely and leave what you can."

I walked through the crowd, stopping to touch the face of a grief-stricken mother and pat the shoulder of a man who had lost a daughter in the raid. "I know you feel broken—I feel the loss too! Comfort one another!"

"Hafa-nu, mekhma!" someone cried out spontaneously.

"Hafa-nu, my people."

"Tonight, I go before you to Egypt! All will be well. All will be well. I go to Pharaoh, but I promise to return to you. And then, my people, we will return to Zerzura! No more wandering in the desert. It is time to go home." The faces of the people lit up with happiness. They whispered to one another. *Yes, home. We must go home. It is time!*

The shock on my uncle's face silenced his consort. This was what had to be done, and I was prepared to do it. There was nothing Omel could do now to take this away from me. I nodded to him in acknowledgement. With his fist over his heart, in the Egyptian way, he acknowledged me. Astora scowled and turned her back on me.

"Hafa-nu, mekhma! Hafa-nu, mekhma!"

I raised both of my hands again as I had seen Farrah do many times. "Hafa-nu, Meshwesh. All will be well." With tears in my eyes, I walked away.

When I awoke and peeped out of my makeshift tent, the Twin Stars were high in the night sky. I took it as a sign—a sign that my sister still lived.

My sister, my own heart. I pray for you this night.

I whispered her name to the Shining Man and asked for his help. I heard nothing and could only hope that he had heard me. Surely he would help me, for I saw him in a dream. He stood atop a tall mountain and stretched his arms out to me, beckoning me to join him. Suddenly I was high above the mountain and could see the entire land. I opened my mouth to say some word, some magical word, but only a scream emerged. It was the scream of a falcon. With supernatural force, I fell from the sky toward the mountain. Surely the Shining Man would catch me! I would be safe! I screamed again, but again the only sound was the falcon's cry. In a flash, the Shining Man disappeared and I stood alone atop the mountain. Startled, I awoke and reached beside me for Alexio, but he had already risen. He was probably preparing the animals for our journey.

My hand flew to my necklace, as if it would protect me from my troubling dreams. There was no time to waste if we were to leave without notice or fanfare. I dug through my scant possessions and rolled up my green silk tunic with the golden embroidery, stuffing it in my bag. I did not want to appear before Pharaoh looking like a goatherd; even I knew the Egyptians had no love for farmers.

I considered visiting my father before I left, but Orba had found the healing herbs that would allow Father to rest; when I last looked, he slept peacefully. He needed healing rest before the arduous journey, and my course lay before me. I knew what needed to be done. After yesterday's speech, I trusted that the Shining Man would give me the words I needed for my audience with Pharaoh. The more I pondered it, the more I believed that. Somehow, I *would* convince Pharaoh to help us. I did not go to him as a pauper but as the Queen of the Meshwesh and a wealthy queen, despite our current situation. We still held the gold and turquoise mines, dozens of horses in Fayyum and stored wealth in many places along the edges of the desert. The only thing we lacked was a home. For far too long, the Meshwesh had been scattered across the Sahara. Since no one oasis could hold us all, the Old Ones, of which Farrah was the last, had agreed to forgo building homes or cities until we could all be together again at Zerzura. Now no one remembered the way.

But there was hope in Egypt. Father told me something I had never known—Egypt knew the way to the White City!

I did not see my uncle either. All that needed to be said to him had been said. I had no desire to visit him before my journey. I would have to trust Orba and the others to keep things in order during my absence. The people were behind me now—they trusted me to help them. I would not fail them.

I heard a noise behind me and turned to greet Alexio. To my surprise it was not my husband who entered but Astora. She knelt down in our makeshift tent and smiled at me.

"Is there something I can do for you, Astora?"

She smiled wider, and it was an unsettling sight. Astora was not a tall woman, but she was pretty—pretty enough to attract the eye of Omel. However, she rarely smiled. She was not Alexio's mother but had been the wife of some minor warrior who lost his life in a Cushite raid some years ago. She had a son, Suri, but I had not seen him since they returned. "No, but I think I can help you." She spoke in an amusing whisper.

"What do you mean? Is this about Omel?"

She laughed and smoothed her gown over her knees. "Where is Alexio? Has he left your bed already? I had hoped to find him here."

I could not stand in my low tent, but I did rise up on my knees. "Get to it. What do you want?"

"I am surprised to see you sharing a bed with a man who has shared his bed with your sister. However, I suppose it is a rare thing to sleep with two mekhmas in one lifetime."

"You lie!" I blurted out.

"Do I?" Her smirk disappeared, and she said savagely, "You're a fool! How do you think we can trust you to lead us if you make such foolish decisions? It is a serious question that many are asking. I only seek to warn you."

"I do not believe you." My mind raced with the possibility. I knew there had been an attraction, at least on Pah's part, but never had I entertained the idea that he might also care for her.

"Why would I lie? Be careful. If you return from Egypt, you could find there is no place for you anymore. Perhaps the days of the mekhma have died, along with the Old One."

"Get out!" I yelled at her.

With a small bow of her head, she disappeared from my tent. One of my guards poked his head in, but I waved him away. I felt my soul crumple under the insinuation. Surely she was wrong. She must be wrong! Images of Pah and Alexio writhing naked together appeared in my mind. Astora's dagger had struck its target. I believed her.

I knew. I guess I had always known.

I grabbed my bag, bow and quiver and stalked through the forlorn camp to Ayn's bed. I knelt down beside her, nudging her side.

"Nefret? I mean, mekhma. What is it?"

"I changed my mind. I want you to go with me."

"Whatever you say. Is Alexio coming too?"

"No, he stays behind. I have another job for him."

She smiled at me and rose from her bed, stretching her back. "I'll be ready in a few minutes. Thank you, mekhma."

"Don't thank me yet. I don't know what is ahead of us. You may regret this."

Before the camp had settled down for sleep the night before, Ayn had come to me and asked to attend me on my journey to Egypt's capital, Thebes. She had apologized again for allowing Paimu out of her sight and expressed her desire to serve me. I had refused to bring her only because I needed strong allies at camp, but now, things had changed.

Everything had changed.

I made my way through the camp as quietly as I could to find Alexio. With all my heart I wanted to scream at him, tear him down, berate him, but I could not do that without stirring up the troubled hearts of my tribesmen. He was where I expected to find him, with his beloved animals. His dark hair hung loose and fell to his shoulders. He tugged at the complicated leather strapping of the camel's harness. Alexio had designed the harness himself, and many riders had been impressed with his ideas. He was a brilliant horseman and camel rider, quick with a blade and his wit. I had loved him since I was a girl, and so had Pah.

"There has been a change of plans," I said flatly. "Ayn is going with me." I tucked my bag into the leather pocket and patted the camel's side, trying to avoid eye contact with Alexio.

"What?" He laughed incredulously. "I can't let you leave alone. My place is by your side. You said so yourself."

"That was before."

Again he laughed. "Before what? Before you went to bed? I just left you, and I remember no change of plans." He tried to take my hand, but I pushed him to the side.

"I can't help what you remember. The plans *have* changed."

He grabbed me gently by my shoulders and turned me around to face him. "What is this about? Have I done something?"

"Take your hands off me," I growled quietly. A nearby watchman stopped his patrol and stared at us. I wasn't used to all this attention. I waved my hand at him, and he passed us by watchfully. I could see Ayn walking toward us in the darkness. I pointed her to the other camel and finally looked at Alexio. "Astora came to visit me."

With an empty sadness, I watched a range of emotions flit across his face. "Oh?"

"Our lives hang in the balance, and you want to play the fool with me? Fine, have it your way. I know about you and Pah. You should have told me before we...you should have told me!" I saw Ayn pause, but she dared not look at us. I knew she heard us, but there was nothing to be done. Nothing was private anymore. I was foolish to think it would be.

"We were never together! I swear to you, Nefret. I did kiss her, but nothing more. Astora has lied to you!"

"You admit to kissing her, toying with her? Then you come to me? She is my sister!"

"I swear to you, I love you, above anyone else. It has always been you. Astora is not innocent—it was she who pursued me, but I refused her. I did kiss Pah, but only that!"

"Keep your voice down."

He took my hand. "Please, believe me. I am sorry that I did not tell you, but I swear to you I love you and you alone. You know that."

I pulled my hand away, climbed on the camel and turned my face away from him, staring into the dark. "I have made up my mind. I do not want you with me. Not now, not ever."

"Please, Nefret. You cannot mean that. What am I supposed to do? How can I prove my love?"

I clucked at the camel for it to stand. "Keep your love!"

"Please! Don't do this."

I stared at him. "If you love me, find my sister. Bring her home." I hardly believed the words I spoke. Again, I felt the presence of the Shining Man; he was somewhere near, but I could not see him. A shudder ran through me. What I was asking of Alexio could be his death sentence. Despite my anger and brokenness, I loved him still. But I would not let this go.

That was not the task he had hoped for, but he did not shirk it.

"If that is your command, mekhma."

"So it is."

Ayn and I rode east away from the camp and into the darkness. I did not look back for fear that I would change my mind.

Chapter Eighteen

The Queen of Egypt—Tiye

It had been a long time since anyone had requested an audience with me except courtiers who were too old to properly bow to me. They came in with their platitudes, mediocre treasures and endless requests, and then out again they streamed. I held the title of chief wife to Pharaoh, but it was in name only now. All of my carefully cultivated influence had slipped carelessly out of my hands and into the lap of Pharaoh's youngest wife and my nemesis, Tadukhipa. I cursed the day that the Mitanni woman entered our world with her strawberry lips and pale skin. Pharaoh needed to scatter his seed—I would have been a fool to imagine otherwise—but the girl forgot her place.

Unlike Pharaoh's previous wives, Tadukhipa had no intention of dwelling in the shadows behind my throne. She was a fool who cared for nothing except pleasure until she fell prey to the schemes of grasping sycophants who easily used her for their own devices. I tried to warn her, guide her, befriend her, but she had responded to my kindness with distrust. By then her ears were full of lies. Then again, she was a stupid girl.

Absently I slid my small silver knife through a crisp pear. I liked the sound of it and the taste. I stared at the juice as it ran down my hand. When I finished slicing it, I tossed a piece into my mouth. A nervous servant waited nearby. Queens should not cut their own fruit, apparently, but I trusted no one in this court anymore, except Huya. How easy it would have been for an enemy to slide a poisoned knife through my green pears!

I sighed as I reviewed all the honors Pharaoh and I had showered upon Tadukhipa. It was I who had sought to raise her status by nicknaming her "The Favorite" and "The Greatly Beloved." My husband allowed me to do as I wished, but no doubt that had been shortsighted on my part. I chuckled as I ate another piece of pear. For her lack of appreciation and respect, I had taken my revenge. Her new nickname, "Kiya" or "the monkey," was the moniker that had finally stuck. She had been furious when she first heard it. It was an obvious poke at her overly large ears and slightly bowed legs. But she did not dare retaliate. I feigned ignorance, but she knew that the insult had been my handiwork.

Unwisely, I had allowed the Monkey to endear herself to my children. It wasn't until she began openly questioning my orders concerning them, going behind my back with my servants, that I suspected her intentions to supplant me. How many times a day had I watched her walk to the Temple of Arinna, her foreign goddess, dressed as a petitioner? Undoubtedly she prayed for my speedy death so that she might rise to the position of Chief Wife, but every day I woke up and defied her and her incompetent deity. There was room for one only queen here and only one goddess worthy of worship! Had she forgotten that I was Isis incarnate?

And now I was forced to watch her work her machinations on my son, the future King of Egypt! It was too much to bear. I would offer Isis a dozen fine oxen this very day if only she would destroy my enemy! I would cut their necks myself!

Now an unknown queen sought audience with me. I was under no obligation to accept her or receive her, but out of curiosity and boredom, I sent my faithful uncle and confidant Huya to appraise the supplicant. I grew tired of watching Kiya parade about the palace as if I were no longer a queen to be feared. I grew bored of this court. I needed some distraction. Huya entered my chamber and pressed his fist against his heart.

"Gracious One, the Meshwesh queen and her attendant wait for you in the Lower Garden."

I wiped my sticky hands and my tiny blade clean with a damp cloth. I slid it back into the folds of my belt and leaned back in the golden chair, propping my aching back against the green cushion. With a sigh, I changed my mind. "I have had enough of lowly queens today, Huya. Send her away."

"Very well, my Queen." He bowed deeply, but I detected his slowness in leaving my presence.

Sensing his resistance to my command, I asked impatiently, "What is it, Huya?"

"If I may…"

"We're too old for formalities," I snapped. "Speak your mind."

With a demure smile he said, "You should see this girl."

I raised a painted eyebrow and leaned forward, curious now. "You seem near to bursting to tell me something." My mind raced with the possibilities. "Is she an Amazon? It has been many years since I have seen one. So strong—so tall!"

How I would have loved to have been given such a strong, glorious body! The gods had a sense of humor. I—the Queen of Upper and Lower Egypt—was no taller than a child, with ugly flat feet, eyes that drooped and a belly that protruded from childbearing. Yes, the gods enjoyed their little jokes. I had no inclinations toward women, as some in the harem (including the Monkey) did, but I valued strength in women above all other things—even honesty.

"No, my Queen. She is no Amazon but has a wild beauty that is rare outside of Thebes and your own radiance."

I snorted, rose from my chair and pulled a fallen linen strap over my bony shoulder. "Well then, let us go see this wild rare beauty. She is in the Lower Garden, you say?"

"Yes, my Queen. Would you like me to bring her into your court?"

"I shall go, but my knees are not as strong as they once were. I hope she is patient."

"You are as strong as ever, Glorious Queen."

I sighed. His lies did not move me as they once had, but I appreciated the effort. "I will steal a look at this flower of the desert. If I find her to be worthy of my attention, I will enter the garden. If not, then send her away."

With a nod and a mysterious smile he pulled back the curtain partition and allowed me to pass through. I shuffled through my painted apartments, ignoring the dozens of faces that offered me greetings or blessings. Fortunately most of the court had filtered into the younger queen's adjoining apartments, no doubt to play games, tell love stories and coddle their children.

After thirty years I barely noticed the white marble columns lining the courtyard that connected us all. I vaguely remembered being entranced by the crocodiles, storks and lotus blossoms on the tile floors beneath my feet. Grecian—no, Roman—tiles, if memory served. What a mess those artisans had made installing them! The smells of juniper incense, orange peels and perfume wafted through the courtyard. I had a sudden longing to see my husband.

It had been too long since Amenhotep had visited his harem—or me. Now that the flux had struck his bowels, he rarely left his palace. I prayed he would return to me soon and set things in order. Far too many liberties were being taken nowadays.

A cool breeze fluttered through the golden curtains that led into the gardens. Beyond the gardens a blue lake sprawled across the horizon, a lake dedicated to me commanded into existence by my husband. I squinted up at Huya, who had emptied the Upper Garden. Apparently word had gotten out about my unexpected visitors. Life ran very still in Pharaoh's harem; any distraction proved an amusement. Once the upper porch was empty, I stepped quietly to the top of the stairs and observed the women below.

The first woman, a dark-haired spear of a girl, disappointed me. She was dressed in dirty brown clothing, and I could almost smell her unwashed skin and hair. I wrinkled my nose.

And then the second girl appeared. Her glorious copper hair tumbled down her back in sparkling waves. Her skin was paler than any Egyptian's, yet it had a lovely bronze glint to it. She was no Amazon, but the queen or whoever she was had a feminine figure with strong arms and dainty feet. She had no crown but wore an impressive gold and emerald necklace around her slender neck, and her arms shone with silver bracelets. Alas, a tribal queen but nothing more. I could tell at first glance.

The world was filled with lovely faces. She even had good bones, but that hair... A definite sign from the gods! No wonder my household clamored for a peek at her. Red hair had long been a mark of divinity. Yes, a sign! Pausing behind a collection of potted palms, I strained to eavesdrop on their conversation. I felt no shame. This was how one learned things, by listening and watching.

"Ayn, calm yourself! You are not helping," the beautiful queen said.

"I am sorry, but I have never seen such things! Even the walls crawl with creatures—and the colors! Have you ever seen such a blue in all your life? And the red! I wish... I wish..." The dirty girl choked up and wiped her eyes.

"What is it?"

"Paimu. She is never far from my thoughts. She would have loved to see all this."

"She is gone, Ayn, and we cannot bring her back. Now a hundred other Paimus depend on us. We cannot act like wide-eyed fools. Please gather yourself and let me think."

"Yes, of course, mekhma. I am sorry."

The desert queen squeezed the girl's hand, and together they strolled about the garden whispering to one another. The redhead comforted her friend as they walked.

I knew their language; it sounded clunky and odd at first, but it came back to my memory quickly. I would never confess to anyone how I knew it. Of all the people in my court, or in Thebes for that matter, only a few remembered how I got here.

Huya, myself and one other.

My mother's scheming had pushed me to this lofty position, but my own will had secured it. Hearing the desert language again made me feel sentimental— sentimental enough to inspect this "queen" more closely.

Without an attendant I stepped lightly down the limestone steps, entering the garden as stealthily as a cat. The plain-faced girl saw me first and froze. The redheaded queen spun about quickly, but I remained poised on the bottom stair with my hands crossed in front of me as I had been trained to do since I was a child. Neither woman knew what to say, so I let them stew in silence for a moment while I took them in and allowed them to view me. I enjoyed making people feel uncomfortable—it was one of the few benefits of being the Queen of Egypt.

"If you want to speak to me, it will have to be alone." The desert dialect fell easily from my lips; it pleased me to see them so surprised at hearing it spoken by an Egyptian queen. *No, I had not forgotten.* I was no longer a wiry child clinging to her mother's legs. The foreign queen dismissed the girl with a gesture. With a hand gesture of her own, the girl walked backwards out of the courtyard, leaving us alone at last.

"Ah, now we are alone. Tell me Queen of the Desert, why are you here? Why did you choose to speak to me?

Wouldn't you rather speak to Pharaoh? He has an eye for beautiful queens. Perhaps my sister-wife, Tadukhipa, could help you. I am merely an old woman with no influence and nothing to offer you."

"But you are the Queen of Egypt! If you cannot help me, no one can. My father, Semkah, sent this to show you. He says you once knew his father, Onesu, and that you would know it."

I felt my hands shake, either from age or from my racing heart. I took the cloth in my hand and sat on the nearby garden bench. Spreading out the rough material with my fingers, I could see the painted symbol—the symbol of the Bee-Eater! A sign of distress, a serious sign to all desert people.

"What is your name?"

To my surprise the girl knelt before me, her hand upraised in the tribal sign of respect. "Great Queen, I am Nefret, daughter of Kadeema of Grecia and Semkah, son of the Red Lands. I am the granddaughter of Onesu, the Warrior-King of Zerzura. I humble myself before you and plead with you for help!" Her passionate speech had her on the brink of tears. I could hear them in her voice. I rose quickly and began to leave.

"Wait! Please!"

I kept my back turned to her. "Have you finished crying?"

"Yes," she sniffled, "I have." I heard the silk of her dress as she hurried to her feet. I returned to my seat and smoothed my dress without making eye contact with her.

"Good. Many years ago, my husband and my pharaoh decreed that tears would never be shed in my presence. He so loves me that he wants me to be happy all the time. May Isis bless him! I cannot stay in the presence of tears. It is the law."

"Great Queen, forgive me. I do not know your laws." She sat on the bench beside me, breaking another law that mandated no one would sit in the presence of the Queen unless invited, but I did not mention it. *She would learn the ways of Egypt. I had almost made up my mind.*

"Tell me about your people, the Meshwesh. Tell me about your home. Tell me what has happened."

She began in a rush, but I calmed her. "No, tell me. Tell me a story. Like the Old Ways." I closed my eyes and leaned back against the wall, waiting. She started slowly, awkwardly, but once she began, her storytelling transported me back in time.

I was again with my own clan, the Algat. Nefret told the *Tale of the Meshwesh*, but it was my own people I thought about. I remembered their faces, so like mine, so foreign to the Egyptian court. The cadence of the girl's gentle voice comforted me as she told me the sad story of the Lightning Gate, the giants and the hidden city. Unlike many of the young people in my court, I believed in the old stories. I remembered them. How simple life had been then! We were too poor to know we were poor, I thought wryly.

As she wove her tale with her sweet, quiet voice, I thought of warm afternoons napping in my tent with my eight sisters. I remembered burrowing under the tent, with my now-dead sister to sneak a peek at the traders who came in daily to see our beautiful women and drink our beer. The Algat brewed the finest beer in the desert, and that was no easy task.

I remembered the nights I spent with my sisters, stealing bits of grilled goat from the spit and scurrying to the tops of trees to see the stars and try to touch them.

How I miss you, Hamrahana, my sister! How I miss you all!

The girl's voice broke my mental wandering: "Another enemy rides against us now and it is time…time to go home to Zerzura where we can defend ourselves." I stared at her face. I noticed that her eye color changed; one minute they were green, in another light they were soft brown—another sign that she had been favored by the gods.

"We lost our way, oh Great Queen. For too long the Meshwesh have been divided, forced to live on oases, never together. Then word came of a wise Queen in the East, the Great Wife of Pharaoh, who once loved and knew the desert people. The Meshwesh, the Algat, the Cushites—all are in danger from the Kiffians, angry men, tall as trees, who ride in secret across the Red Lands—your lands! They steal our women and murder our children. We come to you for justice!"

I grew troubled and considered leaving if only to think. To think and forget again.

"Oh, but more than that, Wise Queen. They want the gold. We have much gold in mines far to the south, more gold than any other clan, and turquoise too." She took a deep breath and said, "As mekhma, I will give you that gold and turquoise, my Queen, if you would only help us. Help us defeat our enemies. Help us find our way home so that we may wander no more. I am only a mekhma—you are the Queen of Lower and Upper Egypt. If you say it will be so, I will believe it. For even more than that, you are also a daughter of the desert."

I sprang out of my seat and walked away, leaving the Desert Queen behind. I had not expected her to identify me so easily. I did not like feeling vulnerable, especially to someone so young and inexperienced.

This morning when the slaves had washed my skin and oiled it with perfumes, I had not thought about my Algat upbringing.

When I broke my fast and dined on the finest eggs, fruits and cold meats, I had not thought of my mother or father. But now all their round faces were before me, and I missed them like I had left them only yesterday.

I missed home. I missed knowing where I belonged.

Amenhotep loved me and I him, but I did not belong here. For thirty years now I had railed against that fact, but it was the truth. Now this Desert Queen had brought those memories back with her storytelling and her shameless pleas for help.

Now, my dear husband, what do I do? It is I who sheds the tears. How can I escape myself?

Chapter Nineteen

The Sun Rises—Nefret

I twisted the corner of my gown nervously and paced the small room I shared with Ayn. The Egyptian court had not been kind to us. We'd been shoved away and told nothing. The Great Wife Tiye had left me in the gardens without so much as a word of warning. I paced the sticky floor and went over the conversation again and again with my friend.

"What will we do now? If they do not let us out of here, I will find a way. We can fight our way out!" Ayn said angrily. She pulled on the door again, but it remained locked as it had all night. Neither of us had slept or eaten. At some point a servant left a tray of unknown meats outside our door, but we refused it. "I should have taken that tray! We would have gotten out then!"

"Keep your voice down, Ayn. We won't get any help here, but we are not beaten yet. Just keep calm. I will see if I can talk to Huya again. He seems a reasonable man."

"Really? What about the Great…"

"Say nothing! Never speak against her! There are many ears here in this palace. We are far from home, Ayn. Very far indeed. Now sit down and rest. We may need it."

As soon as we had a mind to settle down, the door opened and Queen Tiye herself walked in. "Well, Desert Queen, you will have what you asked for. Are you prepared to give me what I want?"

Ayn smiled and stood beside me. I smiled too. "Yes, Great Wife. We give you our gold mines and turquoise. We agree."

"No, that is not what I want. What care I for gold or jewels? I have all I want."

Joy escaped me like the air out of a goat's bladder, a toy we used to play with as a child. "I don't understand. I have nothing else to give."

"For reasons of my own, reasons I do not feel compelled to share with you at this time, I have decided that you can keep your gold and turquoise. Whatever arrangement you have made with my husband, Lord of the Two Lands, is good enough for me. I want something else, Desert Queen."

"What is it you want?"

"I want you. I want you to pledge yourself to me. Pledge that you will stay with me until I die and then when I die, you will stay with my son, Amenhotep."

"What?" I gasped in surprise. I could hardly believe my own ears. Surely I was just tired.

"That is my offer. In exchange for a legion of my soldiers, their provisions and provisions for your people for transport to Zerzura, of which I alone know, I only ask for you."

"Why?" I blurted out.

"As I said, I have my own reasons. What is your answer?"

Ayn looked at me questioningly. I knew what I had to do. I raised my chin defiantly and said, "Yes, I agree. In exchange for all those things, I will stay with you. However, may I ask one thing?"

"You may ask…"

"Give me leave to lead my people to Zerzura. I need to set up my kingdom—I cannot leave it in ruin. My sister, the only other queen, has been abducted by the Kiffians. I need to make sure she is reinstalled as mekhma. Please, I know it is a boon to ask it."

The short queen frowned, but she nodded, closing her heavy eyelids once. "So be it. Huya will make all the arrangements and come for you in three days. In the meantime, you will dine with me at all meals. Leave your servant behind. A room has been prepared for you in my apartments."

I bowed, bending my knees slightly. "I am grateful. Thank you." With a flurry of servants, she left me again. Only this time, the door was left open.

"I want you to go, Ayn. Go back to Saqqara and tell my uncle what has happened. No—wait! Don't tell him that I must return to Egypt. Just tell him that I have made the provisions. Yes, that is all he needs to know for now."

"Wise decision, but I do not like this, Nefret. I can't leave you—not now! What does she want with you? Can she really hold you here?"

"Oh yes, she can. Don't worry for me, Ayn. I will ride back with you. Perhaps the Shining Man will come to me and show me a new path to walk."

"What? Who?"

With a sigh, I sat on the bed with my head in my hands. I wanted to cry, sleep and cry some more.

"Nothing. It's nothing. Go, Ayn. I will meet you at Saqqara when I bring the Egyptians."

"Very well, mekhma." She paused in the doorway and smiled at me, "One day, this will be a story. *The Tale of Nefret*, we will call it. A story of a great mekhma who gave everything for her people. Yes, I will tell that story. I promise."

I nodded and let the tears flow. Ayn stayed with me until I fell asleep.

I awoke with the immediate awareness that I was completely alone and everything had changed.

I would never be the same.

Read on for an excerpt from The Falcon Rises,
Book 2 of The Desert Queen Series

"Well," Kiya said, sniffing the air as if she detected something foul, "what is this terrific smell? Camel dung? Is that the new scent from the exotic desert?"

Her game partner, Meritamon, shook the amber dice and studied the board before moving a marble game piece. Absently she answered, "Too earthy for me. What about you, Inhapi?"

The third woman did not speak but pretended to gag as she held her fingers over her nose and shook her head. The trio broke out into giggles. Anger whipped up within me like a desert wind. I let the silver bowl full of citrus fruits crash to the ground. It made a terrible clatter, and bright oranges bounced across the courtyard. Kiya sprang to her feet. "You pick that up, stupid!"

I stared at her with all the hatred I could muster. It was time to end this. I'd had enough of her snide comments. Very easily I could beat her to death with the bowl that lay at my feet.

"Never," I whispered ferociously. "I am not your slave!"

"Then I shall have you whipped like the goat that you are! How dare you defy me—I am the wife of Amenhotep! Pick up that tray, now!"

Before she could speak another word, Huya stepped out of the shadows from his hiding place along the outer wall. He was always lurking about. I had not noticed him before. He said nothing but merely stared at us. *Do not do what you are thinking*, his eyes warned me. I do not know what warning Kiya saw in his stare, but it held her anger at bay—at least for the moment.

The reality of my situation struck me as soundly as I imagined striking Kiya.

I was never leaving Egypt.

I had achieved the dream of all mekhmas. I had led the Meshwesh back to Zerzura, but there my story ended. With my sister now ruling in my stead and Alexio at her side, there was nothing left for me to return to. I knew the truth of the matter—my star had fallen, my destiny had changed. I would never see Zerzura or any of my tribe again.

Yet despite it all, I lived. I remembered Queen Tiye's words to me before she left for Thebes, "You can live as a prisoner, or you can become a true Queen. Those are your choices. There is nothing else."

I would not live as a prisoner, nor would I be Kiya's fool. I made my decision.

I took a deep breath and picked up the tray from the floor. As I picked up each piece of fruit I made a resolution. I would condition my mind—I would never think of Alexio, Pah or my father or any of the other Meshwesh again. I would not cry over them or burn incense to any foreign gods for direction and favor.

I knew what I wanted—what I must do.

I would become queen of all Egypt. I would truly become Nefertiti.

Read more from M.L. Bullock

The Seven Sisters Series

Seven Sisters
Moonlight Falls on Seven Sisters
Shadows Stir at Seven Sisters
The Stars that Fell
The Stars We Walked Upon

The Desert Queen Series

The Tale of Nefret
The Falcon Rises
The Kingdom of Nefertiti (forthcoming)
The Song of the Bee-Eater (forthcoming)

The Sirens Gate Series (forthcoming)

The Mermaid's Gift
The Blood Feud
The Wrath of Minerva
The Lorelei Curse
The Fortunate Star

The Southern Gothic Series

Being with Beau

To receive updates on her latest releases,
visit her website at MLBullock.com
and subscribe to her mailing list.

About the Author

Author of the best-selling *Seven Sisters* series, M.L. Bullock has been storytelling since she was a child. A student of archaeology, she loves weaving stories that feature her favorite historical characters—including Nefertiti. She currently lives on the Gulf Coast with her family but travels frequently to exotic locations around the globe.

Made in the USA
Middletown, DE
14 July 2018